# POLLY'S CHOICE

## PIONEER BRIDES OF THE OREGON TRAIL

## INDIANA WAKE

FAIR HAVENS BOOKS

## WALKING AND ROMANCE ON THE OREGON TRAIL

As with each of these books I want to tell you a little bit about the time and place that I'm writing about. To give you a little flavour of life on the Trail.

Traveling the Oregon Trail was a long slow process. At 2170 it was a mammoth journey mostly traveled on foot. The Prairie Schooner wagons were small and loaded with equipment, belongings and food. There was no room for passengers unless illness forced a small space to be cleared.

The pioneers would walk about 15 miles a day alongside the wagons. Sometimes they would need to push or dig the wagons out. Sometimes they would need to lighten the load to cross rivers or to get up steep inclines.

If the journey was not timed to perfection and the grass was not enough to feed the oxen then they would need to leave belonging along the trail.

At first the excitement would keep them going but the trip became tedious and so love and romance were a big part of the journey.

Weddings were often performed along the route. Weddings in the camps were not uncommon and sometimes would be performed at trading posts such as Platte River or Fort Laramie.

Births were also common place midwives would often be present they were special and celebrated as were the marriages but time was limited and they would soon be moving once again.

Polly's Choice is the forth book I have written about women who travel the Oregon Trail looking for a new future. Each book is a complete story and they can be read in any order.

The first book was Trinity's Loss http://amzn.to/2xrn4B5

The second is Carrie's Trust http://amzn.to/2wGi86k

The Third is Josie's Dream http://amzn.to/2xXaxp8

To receive two free Mail Order Bride Romance join Fair Havens Books exclusive newsletter. http://eepurl.com/bHou5D

God bless,

*Indiana Wake*

## CHAPTER 1

"*J*'m so glad you came today, Polly. Not just because I made more apple pie than I can eat, but because I thought you looked so downcast last time I saw you." Trinity Goodman smiled as she cut two immense slices from the as yet untouched apple pie.

The two were sitting in Trinity Goodman's brand-new kitchen in her brand-new home. Her husband, Dillon, had made a good job of the place, building it immediately after he had his business up and running.

"I guess I've been down in the dumps for a little while now. I'm just missing Travis, you know?" While this was true, Polly Whitaker knew that there was so much more to be said.

She wasn't giving Trinity the whole truth, and she knew it. Sure, she missed Travis; she missed him so badly it was like a physical pain in her chest. But there was more to it than simply waiting for him, much more.

"Have you heard anything this week?" Trinity had a really

kind way about her to find out whatever she needed to, but Polly knew she was no gossip.

Trinity just cared, and that was all.

When Polly had bumped into Trinity in the grocery store just a few weeks before, she'd recognized her immediately from the wagon train. She remembered Trinity more from the early part of the arduous journey across the Oregon Trail. Anything after that seemed a blur, and whenever she tried to recall the details of the rest of the journey, all she could see was Travis Hurst.

As the two women had locked eyes in the grocery store, Trinity smiled broadly and called her by name. To Polly's shame, she couldn't remember Trinity's name at all, if she had ever known it in the first place.

Still, none of that had bothered Trinity, just as bright and friendly as ever. She had been instantly keen to find out how Polly had been doing, and had even asked about Travis. She seemed to know all about their sad, if temporary, parting. Polly found herself a little taken aback. Obviously, Trinity was a very much more observant person than she was. Not to mention the fact that she seemed to have a great capacity for caring for people, even if they were practically strangers.

"No, I haven't heard a thing from him," Polly said, the familiar sense of foreboding gripping her heart.

"Just nothing this week, or nothing at all?" Trinity spoke cautiously, obviously keen not to upset her.

"Nothing at all." Polly had been about to raise a fork full of apple pie to her mouth, lowered it again and rested her fork on her plate.

"Are you alright, honey?" Trinity's face was that of concern and was absolutely genuine.

"Not really," Polly said truthfully. "But I'm real determined not to cry."

"You're with a friend now, Polly. You can cry all you want to, if that's how you feel. Don't you go holding back on my account." Trinity was so kind that Polly struggled to hold back her tears.

However, she reckoned she'd cried enough lately, albeit in the privacy of her own room, in the farmhouse that her father had built up so quickly when they had arrived in Oregon.

"That's so kind of you, Trinity. I wish I got to know you better out there, out on the trail," Polly said, a little chagrined. "Instead of being wrapped up in my own world, Travis, and what have you."

"You were in love, that's all," Trinity said with a laugh. "And when it hits you, you can't always concentrate on everything else. To be honest, you were probably better off being in your own little world on that journey. At least when you look back, you'll remember the love and the dancing and the singing, and not the mud and the rivers and the Rocky Mountain pass." She finished with a warm smile.

"And yet, now I wish I had something else to think about." Polly paused for a moment. "I'm sorry, I guess that sounds real selfish. Especially after everything that you went through out there, you must think me nothing more than a silly little lovelorn girl."

"I think nothing of the sort." Trinity tapped her plate with her fork and raised her eyebrows, indicating that her friend

3

should eat her pie. "And I was all set to fall in love with Dillon out there on the trail before things went wrong. I know we got together in the end, but I would have been as lovelorn as you out there in the same circumstances. Don't be so hard on yourself, you're human."

"And I guess we can't change what's in the past, can we?"

"Would you really want to change any of it?" Trinity asked gently.

"Maybe."

"Is there something you're not telling me about Travis?"

"There is." Polly's voice was so strained she hardly recognized it herself. "I guess I can't help thinking that Travis really isn't going to come for me." It felt so hard, so harsh, to hear the words out loud.

"And he's never written to you at all? I mean, you haven't had one letter in all the time that you've been here in Oregon?" Trinity reached out across the table and took Polly's hand.

"No." Polly felt a thickening in her throat and tried to swallow it down.

When she first arrived in Oregon with her mother and father, Polly had been sad, but also excited at the same time. In her heart, she had known that Travis Hurst, her first and only love, would be back for her soon.

All it would take was a little while, time enough for him to start earning money in the gold mines of California and get a place of his own. As soon as that was done, she knew that he would come for her. After all, that's what he'd promised.

Trinity had met Travis within days of setting off from Independence, Missouri, on the Oregon Trail. Travis didn't have much with him, no wagon, livestock, or farming equipment. It was just Travis on his horse with a laden pack carrying all his worldly possessions.

Trinity had spotted him almost immediately. He was so handsome and so big he could hardly be missed. Travis was tall and broad, the perfect build for a farmer or a rancher, and he had the lightest, sun-kissed blonde hair and brown skin. His eyes were twinkly blue and his smile held just enough mischief to make him a little bit dangerous.

"Hey, you want to go up on my horse for a while?" Was the first thing he'd ever said to her.

The Whitaker family wagon was loaded to capacity and, unless somebody was feeling unwell, neither she nor her parents rode in the wagon during the day. They simply walked alongside Clarence Whitaker, urging his oxen along while his wife and daughter kept him company on foot.

After the first couple of days, Angela Whitaker, Polly's mother, had realized that Polly would not disappear without a trace if she simply wandered off and made friends along the way. And the very moment that Polly sensed her mother relax, she'd made a pretty good point of hanging back a little and giving an eye to the handsome young horseman who seemed to be watching her as much as she was watching him.

"But won't your legs get tired?" Polly had smiled at him.

"No, my legs will be just fine. Here, let me help you up." Without waiting for her answer, he lifted her up onto the horse.

He lifted her so quickly and easily it was as if she weighed no more than a child. He was so strong, and Polly was instantly impressed, her mind already filling with romantic notions.

"My name's Travis Hurst," he said, lifting his broad brim hat just a little as he looked up at her. "What's yours?" By the way he smiled, Polly knew that he was as interested in her as she was in him, and the idea of it gave her butterflies in her stomach.

Now, when Polly thought of those first few days, it did not fortify her the way it had done when she first arrived in Oregon. Now it simply made her sad, reminding her of everything she had lost. Or at least everything she thought, and feared she had lost.

"Polly, did he actually say that he would write? I mean, some men aren't too good at that sort of thing, are they?" Trinity said, and Polly knew that she was trying to keep her spirits up.

"I appreciate that, Trinity." Polly smiled, feeling the warmth of her friend's care. "But it didn't need to be a long letter, did it? Just a few lines to let me know that he'd arrived in California safely and that he still loved me. That was all I needed, really."

"I understand, and I am so sorry."

"I think I've been lying to myself for a good long while now. I haven't really allowed myself to imagine that Travis is never coming. Every day I go down to the mail office and ask if there's anything for me, any letters at all. And every day my heart sinks. I know now, even as I'm walking to the mail office, that there won't be anything. I know he won't have written. And yet, I still go. I can't let myself believe that it's all over." Polly's voice had leveled, and she was surprised that she had been able to speak the truth out loud without crying.

"Maybe he just hasn't been able to write to you for some

reason," Trinity said thoughtfully. "He might have had an accident or hit some other misfortune."

"There were enough guys riding along with him to California who knew that I'd be waiting for him. I can't believe that something could have happened to Travis and not one of them would have got word to the mail office here in Oregon."

"I guess that makes sense." Trinity nodded slowly. "And it's comforting in its own way, I suppose. I mean, at least you know he's alright."

"Yes, if nothing else, I'm certain that he's alright."

"What do you think has happened?"

"Trinity, I can't help wondering if he's settled upon some girl down in California. Someone pretty or smarter than me."

"Now, don't you go comparing yourself to some woman who probably doesn't even exist," Trinity said with a warm kind of sharpness. "Sure, you might wonder if he's found somebody else by now, that's only natural. But there's no need to run yourself down because of it, really there isn't. You're already smart and pretty, and you don't need to doubt that for a moment, alright?"

"That's kind of you, Trinity. I sure am glad that we bumped into one another in the grocery store when we did. I'm glad I got the chance to get to know you finally, and I don't know what I'd do without you now. I don't like to talk my fears over with my mama and daddy, they have enough to do. They've worked so hard to get the farm up and running that the last thing they need is to see me looking so downcast and feeling sorry for myself."

"Polly, I'm sure they wouldn't see it that way. I'm sure your mama already knows that you're feeling low and she's just waiting for you to say something."

"Yes, you're probably right."

"Look, why don't I give you something else to concentrate on for a little while?" Trinity said with a smile.

"But what?"

"I want you to come with me to the town barn dance next week. I think it would do you good to get out for a while and enjoy yourself, think about something else other than Travis Hurst." Trinity's smile had grown broader and broader. She was clearly looking forward to the barn dance herself. "Dillon is coming, but he usually finds somebody to get talking to, so we'd have time for dancing and gossiping. What do you say?"

"Alright," Polly said, nodding and slowly beginning to smile. "And maybe you're right, maybe it will lift me out of my own gloom for a little while. Thank you, Trinity."

## CHAPTER 2

"You've certainly caught somebody's eye," Trinity said loudly over the music of half a dozen fiddlers.

"Do you mean that man over there talking to Dillon?" Polly said with a frown.

"I sure do."

"I thought so." Polly stared over at the man with a flat expression.

Dillon had wandered off sometime before to speak to so many different people that Polly could hardly keep track. He was a popular man, friendly and funny, so it was no surprise that he easily found company.

But he ran the newly opened merchant store too, and Polly thought it likely that several of the men who spoke to him for two or three minutes at a time, wanted to ask him something business related. Perhaps there was something they needed and wondered if he could start having it shipped in and distributed to one of the smaller stores.

Those conversations were easy enough to spot, and so Polly could tell that the man Dillon had been talking and laughing with for more than half an hour was undoubtedly a friend. And the friend seemed unable to take his eyes off her.

Before Polly had ever met Travis, such attention would have made her cheeks flush and her heart beat with excitement. After all, the young man who was staring over at her was certainly handsome. He was tall and broad, although not as tall and broad as Travis, and his hair was very dark indeed. He had tanned skin and a nice smile and, since she could hear it from across the barn, he had a pleasing, humorous laugh.

"You don't seem too happy about it, Polly," Trinity said gently.

"I'm sorry, Trinity. I don't mean to be so sour-faced, and it certainly isn't that poor man's fault. I guess I'm just not ready to let go of Travis. I know I said that I don't think he'll ever come, but there is still a part of me that can't quite give up on him yet. There's a part of me that wants to give him a little more time, if that makes sense."

"It makes perfect sense, Polly. But it doesn't mean that you can't make friends, does it?"

"I guess not," Polly said, trying to be accommodating, but truly feeling anything but joy in the situation.

The very idea of speaking to the young man made her feel uneasy, as if she would be betraying Travis in some way. Despite the fact she had been torturing herself for days with the idea that Travis had now settled down with another, still, she couldn't quite bring herself to move on with her own life. After all, Travis might not have done any such thing. He might be, even then, being utterly true to her.

To Polly's horror, Dillon was making his way back over to his wife, bringing the young man with him. Suddenly, Polly felt as if she had been set up, even though she knew she hadn't, that Trinity would never do that.

Still, she felt trapped, and suddenly wanted to turn and run from the barn; she just wasn't ready for this.

"How are you girls doing?" Dillon asked with his customary bright smile.

"I reckon we're doing just fine, honey." Trinity smiled to her husband with warmth.

"Polly, may I introduce you to a good friend of mine? This is Gavin Swain." Dillon looked from Polly to Gavin Swain and back again.

"Of course," Polly said with every bit of good manners she could muster. "It's a pleasure to meet you, Mr. Swain." She smiled at the stranger.

"And it's a real pleasure to meet you, Miss Whitaker." Gavin smiled at her and she saw something there that she thought, for a moment, she recognized.

"Gavin came over the Oregon Trail last year, Polly," Dillon said, seemingly determined to keep the conversation going. "He's a farmer out on the east side of things, the opposite side from your daddy's farm."

"Well, that's nice," Polly said in a noncommittal fashion.

"And how are you finding things here in Oregon?" Gavin

spoke to her directly, and she realized why she'd got such a flash of recognition.

Gavin had eyes as blue and bright as Travis had, although they seemed to stand out even more brightly against his dark hair. But not only that, Gavin had an air about him, something in his smile which suggested a little mischief, a kind of zest for life.

Although he really looked nothing like Travis, there was a vitality about Gavin Swain which reminded her of him and reinforced the idea, somehow, that she was betraying Travis.

"I'm finding things just nice, Mr. Swain, thank you." Polly tried to sound cheerful but could hear the clipped edge to her tone. "My daddy's farm is up and running already. He's worked real hard on it and so I suppose life is just beginning."

"A whole new chapter, I guess. And I guess it's the same for all of us out here now." Gavin smiled and looked at her intently, letting her know that he was very pleased with what he saw.

"I guess so." Although she didn't want to be rude, Polly was determined not to be overly conversational.

After all, she didn't want to encourage Gavin Swain, she didn't want him to think that she was interested in him in the way that he was clearly interested in her.

"So, who's up for a dance then?" Trinity asked excitedly when the fiddlers struck up a vigorous tune and the crowd cheered.

"Alright, come on then," Dillon said with a laugh as he took his wife's hand.

"What about you, Miss Whitaker?" Gavin said and looked at her hopefully.

"No, not this time," Polly said and gave him a frozen smile.

Trinity's face fell a little and Polly realized that her friend really was looking forward to a dance. She wasn't trying to edge Polly into dancing with Gavin at all.

"But don't let that stop you," Polly said with a brighter smile. "I want to see you both out there giving it your all, Mr. and Mrs. Goodman." Polly chuckled in the hope of easing the tension that she realized she had created.

"So, why is it a young woman with her health and strength and a pretty dress in the middle of a barn dance doesn't want to dance?" Gavin Swain asked with a laugh the moment Trinity and Dillon had departed for the dance floor.

"I just don't feel like it," Polly snapped.

"There is no need to bite my head off," Gavin said, but laughed good-naturedly. "I reckon I already realized that you weren't too keen to be introduced to me."

"I'm sorry," Polly said, feeling truly shabby about the way she'd dealt with him. "I guess I'm not in the best of moods tonight."

"I'd ask, but you seem kind of tense." Gavin looked at her and she saw the mischievous expression. "Like you could knock me out with one punch or something."

"Oh, for goodness sake!" Polly said, and laughed despite herself.

"Ah, now that's better." Gavin took a drink of his beer. "You're even prettier when you smile."

13

"Well that's nice of you to say, but it won't do you any good," Polly said, deciding that she would clearly need to be forthright with this young man.

"And why is that?" He was grinning at her.

"Because I already have somebody, Mr. Swain."

"Well, I guess that's a real shame for me." He smiled and shrugged and she was surprised when he continued to stand there. "But hardly a surprise with a beautiful girl like you."

"Well, you don't give up easily, do you?" Polly felt herself relax a little now that she had roughly explained her circumstances.

"I don't give up at all." Gavin laughed. "But still, it doesn't mean that we can't talk, does it? I reckon when you come to a new place like this you need as many friends as you can lay your hands on. What do you say?"

"To being your friend, Mr. Swain?"

"Yes. And please, call me Gavin. Mr. Swain makes me feel old and I'm not much older than you." He grinned again.

"Well, I guess there's no harm in being your friend. But as long as you don't keep looking at me like that."

"Like what?" Gavin spread his hands wide and started to chuckle, low and deep.

"Like that!" Polly said in an exasperated tone. "You know exactly what I mean."

"Don't worry, as pretty as you are, I don't go trying to steal young ladies off their menfolk. I like my face just the way it is, nose, eyes, and mouth all in alignment."

"Well, in that case, we can be friends." Polly was suddenly greatly amused by him.

Gavin had an openness about him that was very appealing and she thought that he would, in the end, make a nice kind of a friend. He would make her laugh, if nothing else. And as long as he didn't try to woo her in any way, maybe they'd be just fine.

"So, I can call you Polly then?" He tipped his head to one side, his eyes meeting hers. "Because if I keep calling you Miss Whitaker, I'll feel like I'm a little boy back in the schoolroom learning to read."

"I'm just glad to hear that you learned something in the schoolroom," Polly said, teasing him a little. "Because you strike me as a sort of man who would have made a very cheeky little boy, one who didn't concentrate much on his lessons."

"You've got me pegged just right, Polly." He laughed. "And I'm probably still kind of a cheeky little boy sometimes too. Just you learn to take me with a pinch of salt and you won't be so offended by me."

"Well, that's advice I will take, Gavin." She laughed.

"So, now that you're smiling, what about a dance?"

"No, I still don't want to dance," Polly said, and felt the humor leave her.

She'd begun to warm to Gavin, not in any romantic sense, but just because he was such a bright and friendly man. But still it seemed like too much, almost as if she feared that Travis would walk into the barn at any moment and see her there with another man.

"Well, never mind." He didn't protest and Polly was glad of it. "I'll just settle for keeping you company for a while."

"Thank you."

"Well, why don't you tell me a little something of the lucky man who's managed to win your affections, Polly?" Gavin didn't seem at all envious, rather he seemed genuinely interested.

"His name is Travis," Polly said, and wondered how she was going to explain it all out to him.

"And is he a farmer too?" Gavin asked when Polly went silent.

"No, he's a miner."

"Gold?" Gavin said with raised eyebrows. "Or coal?"

"Gold," Polly said, but realized that she didn't truly know if that was what Travis was doing now.

After all, without any word from him, for all that she knew he could be doing anything. He might never have found work at the goldmines, although that seemed unlikely in California.

"Not here in Oregon, though?" Gavin said, and Polly studied him closely.

It was clear that he had realized that Polly's love was not in town and, for a moment, she wondered if that would give him the idea that she was worth making a try for. However, when she looked into his face, she could see no sign of pleasure at the idea that she was alone.

"No, he's down in California."

"I thought as much." Gavin nodded thoughtfully. "I reckon that is the place the gold is these days."

"I reckon it is."

"Well, I'm going to grab me another drink. Why don't I bring you one too?"

Polly was pleased that Gavin hadn't questioned her any further. Maybe he'd sensed that it was something she just didn't want to discuss. Either way, she was pleased that he had abandoned the subject in favor of fetching them both drinks instead.

# CHAPTER 3

*J*ust days after the barn dance, Polly took the horse and cart down into the town to collect provisions, just as she did once or twice every week.

Enjoying the break from their home on the edge of things, Polly had offered herself as the person who would predominantly go into town to collect their supplies. And she never particularly hurried, liking the bustle of the town, all stores and businesses and life.

Not to mention the fact that Trinity and Dillon's plot was down in the town, just on the edge. Dillon was always busy with supplies and orders and, when she wasn't helping him, Trinity almost always had time for a break and a drink and, more often than not, a little gossip.

Polly was still in the grocery store giving the last of her order when she decided that she would make her way over to the Goodman place to see if Trinity was free for half an hour. She'd just get the cart loaded and be on her way.

"Can I help you with that?" Gavin Swain seemed to appear from nowhere and, without waiting for her answer, took the small sack of flour out of her arms. "Is that your cart out front?"

"Yes, yes it is." Polly was somewhat taken aback, not having given the young man a moment's thought since the barn dance.

In the end, she passed a pleasant evening and had found Gavin funny and talkative. All in all, he'd been very good company. But she had not been able to shake thoughts of Travis throughout the evening and those thoughts seemed to have grown in intensity in the days which followed, almost as if she was subconsciously trying to tell herself that she had done nothing to betray the man she loved.

While Gavin disappeared out of the store to put the bag of flour into the back of the cart, the grocer smiled at her and set out everything else that she had ordered on the counter. When Gavin returned, the grocer pointed out the rest of it with a grin.

"Is this all yours too?" Gavin asked, his eyes wide when he realized what he'd let himself in for.

"It sure is," Polly said, highly amused. "But that's just fine, Gavin, I can do it." She teased.

"No, no," Gavin said, and set to ferrying the goods out to the cart to the accompaniment of the light laughter of the grocer.

"What us men won't do to impress a pretty girl," The grocer said to her in confidential, amused tones.

"Oh, he's just a friend," Polly said, although she could see that the grocer didn't believe it for a minute.

When Gavin had finished loading the cart, he came back into the grocery store and smiled at her.

"Well, what do you say to a nice cup of coffee over at Mrs. Taplow's diner?" He said with a bright smile, the tiny beads of sweat on his handsome face giving testimony to his hard work.

"Oh, I don't know," Polly said, a minor sense of panic overcoming her. "I mean, I had thought of going over to see Trinity for a little while."

"Well, a cup of coffee will only take ten minutes, maybe eleven." Gavin was smiling at her and holding his arms out to the sides appealingly.

Polly was torn. On the one hand, she still felt the same sense of obligation to Travis and yet, on the other, she thought that she ought really to spend a few minutes with the man who had gone out of his way to load her cart. And, of course, she hadn't made any actual arrangement with Trinity to go and see her. She had simply decided on a whim and so there would be no harm, not really, in going to Mrs. Taplow's diner with Gavin instead.

Polly knew, deep down, that Gavin was still interested in her. But she also knew that he had accepted the terms of their friendship, and she felt certain that he wouldn't breach them in any way. She was quite safe in his company, and she knew it. And Gavin had been absolutely right when he said that a person needed friends, especially in a new town. Apart from Trinity and Dillon, Polly didn't really see anybody else, excepting the store owners in town.

The truth was that she'd been too wrapped up in thoughts of Travis to find friends of her own. She just assumed that, sooner or later, Travis would come for her and take her back to California with him. Her friends, her new friends, would all be there, surely.

But now, now that she was not as confident as once she was, Trinity had begun to feel a little lonely at times. And what would be the harm in spending ten, *or eleven*, minutes with a man who knew she wanted nothing more than friendship?

"Alright then, but I've only got *eleven* minutes," Polly said with a smile.

As she turned to bid farewell to the grocer, she noted his knowing smile but decided against making any sort of protestation in front of Gavin.

"If you eat real quick, we've got time for a slice of pie too. I think it will still keep us safely inside our eleven minutes, Polly." Gavin chuckled when they were settled down in a corner booth in the diner.

"That sounds nice. And I suppose if it stretches to twelve minutes, there'd be no harm done." Polly found it very easy to get into the spirit of Gavin's light-hearted ways.

"You sure are a generous woman." He was both amused and amusing, and Polly studied him a little more closely as he turned in his seat and tried to get the attention of Mrs. Taplow.

Gavin really was a strangely handsome man. There was a lack of symmetry in his features which, in anybody else, might not have been attractive at all. His smile was gently lopsided and his nose just a little crooked, and yet it gave him character.

Polly thought that it was, perhaps, his confidence and his open nature which made him handsome. After all, he wasn't the sort of man that she would have gone out of her way to make eye contact with on the Oregon Trail, just as she had with Travis. Travis was much more traditionally handsome, every one of his features perfect, proportionate, and exactly where it ought to be.

Travis was the sort of man who caught every girl's eye, Polly had always known that. But Gavin was a different sort of man altogether, a man who became more handsome as you got to know him.

Polly managed to catch Mrs. Taplow's eye before Gavin did and, with a smile, beckoned her over. She hurriedly ordered for them both, apple and berry pie and coffee, and Mrs. Taplow set off immediately. Gavin looked at her and then at Mrs. Taplow's retreating back, his nose wrinkling comically.

"Well, I thought if I didn't do something soon you might keel over. After all, you sure have exerted yourself this morning loading my cart and all."

"How did you manage to get her attention?" Gavin said, mock surprise on his face. "I mean, you're pretty and all, but to Mrs. Taplow, I ought to be devastatingly handsome."

Polly couldn't think of a thing to say and simply burst out laughing. Gavin had a wonderful, completely silly sense of humor, and it was very hard not to be pulled along in its wake.

"Mrs. Taplow is a grandmother, Gavin," Polly said, still laughing. "Anybody under the age of thirty is devastatingly handsome in her eyes, I'm sure."

"Now I can't work out if you're insulting me or Mrs. Taplow."

"Neither," Polly said with a chuckle. "I'm just teasing. I'm sure Mrs. Taplow thinks you're a real nice young man."

"You know, when a man first meets you, you're kind of misleading." He began a little cautiously.

"How so?" Polly was not sure she wanted the conversation to take a serious turn.

"Well, you were frostier than a New York winter when I first met you. As pretty as you are, I couldn't imagine for a minute that you had a sense of humor at all."

"Is this supposed to be flattering in any way?" Polly said, shaking her head from side to side, smiling and relieved that the subject was not too serious after all.

"Probably not." He chuckled. "But it's actually true. I could feel the temperature drop as I made my way across the barn towards you."

"Well, I guess I was just a little out of sorts." Polly defended herself light-heartedly, but knew that she had been truly standoffish.

"I suppose it would be prying to ask if it had anything to do with that man of yours?"

"Yes, it would be prying," Polly said, but smiled at him nonetheless.

There was just something about Gavin; now that she knew him just a little better, it seemed almost impossible to be annoyed with him. *It didn't bode well*, she thought, *if it meant that he could get away with all sorts of things.*

"Right. I *thought* it would be prying." Gavin said and nodded vigorously. "So, were you out of sorts about that man of yours?" He grinned, undeterred.

"Well, I suppose you did say that you don't give up." Polly laughed. "And yes, I just miss him," she said honestly.

"I'm assuming that you haven't seen him since the Parting of the Ways?"

"No, I haven't seen him since then." She almost said that she hadn't heard from him either.

Polly could hardly believe she had been about to part with such a confidence, especially to a man who had already claimed some sort of interest in her.

"So, when he comes for you, I take it you'll be heading off to California?"

"I guess so," Polly said with a shrug. "Travis didn't reckon he could take to farming. He didn't come from a farming background and he thought he would make faster money in the mines."

"Well, I guess that's true. You need a little bit behind you to get going on farming in a new place. Especially on un-farmed land that needs turning and getting right, not to mention building a home too." Gavin shrugged.

"And you're all up and running now, are you?" Polly said, keen to take the emphasis off Travis for a while.

"Yes, everything is ticking over nicely now. And I have a nice little farmhouse on my land too. You could come over and see it sometime if you wanted." Gavin smiled a little ruefully.

"Well, it's nice to know that things are working out of you," Polly said, not committing herself.

"So, when do you think that Travis will be coming for you? It must be eight months now since your wagon train rolled in?" Gavin seemed determined to return to the subject of Travis.

"Yes, I guess it is," Polly said, the old familiar feeling of loss washing over her once more. "And Travis will be along for me just as soon as he has settled things there. He wanted to get everything just right." Polly could hear the uncertainty herself.

"Forgive me, Polly, you don't sound so sure."

"So sure of what?" She said a little angrily.

"I don't know, there's just something in your eyes."

"Gavin, that doesn't make sense," she said, and determined to change the subject again. "I wonder what's taking Mrs. Taplow with that pie."

"It's like you don't really believe it yourself." Gavin said, completely ignoring her trying to avoid the conversation

"Don't believe what?" Polly was really scrabbling about for something to say while, at the same time, trying to keep her temper in check.

"You don't believe he's coming for you, do you?" Gavin said, and it was the most serious she had ever seen him.

"That's not true, Gavin." Polly pushed her chair back, and began to rise to her feet.

"Hey, where are you going?" Gavin said, his eyes wide and his mouth hanging open just a little.

"I can't believe you would say something like that." Polly was genuinely annoyed, but annoyed that Gavin had seen right into her heart more than anything else. "Of course, Travis is coming for me. We love each other, and we always will." She turned to leave.

"Well, that's just great," Gavin said, his face a picture of apology. "I'm sorry I said it."

"I'm going to go now. I need to get back to the farm, anyway," Polly said and couldn't quite look at him.

She didn't really want Gavin to see what she knew would be there in her eyes. If he looked at her now, if he stared into her eyes, he would see the doubt so clearly.

"Polly, don't go. Look, Mrs. Taplow is bringing our food."

"Well, you eat it." Polly snapped and marched out of the diner.

# CHAPTER 4

"*W*ell, you seem to be of the same opinion as Trinity, if I'm honest," Dillon said as he lifted another heavy sack of seed and set off to store it in its rightful place. "If you're going to follow me, Gavin, bring one of those sacks with you," he laughed.

Gavin picked up one of the sacks, groaning a little as he did so. It really was very heavy indeed. As he followed along behind Dillon, he began to heartily wish that he hadn't arrived at the merchant store just as an immense seed delivery had been made.

"I just think that this Travis Hurst, or whatever his name is, must have decided never to come for her. I mean, surely eight months is long enough for a man to get himself settled somewhere, especially if he's just gold mining. Just a matter of getting a job, isn't it? I mean, it's not like farming where you have to put a lot of effort in before you start turning a buck." Gavin dropped the heavy sack on the spot Dillon indicated.

"Thanks," Dillon said, and then sat down on the sack that Gavin had just dropped. "And you're right, it is just a case of getting a job and getting a place. To be honest, if he was that dead set on the girl, why didn't he just take her with him in the first place? It wouldn't have been the first marriage made on the Oregon Trail after all, would it?"

"You make a good point, Dillon. I reckon I agree with that one," Gavin said thoughtfully. "I mean, if I'd been him, if I'd been Travis Hurst, I wouldn't have let her go."

"My friend, you seem to be getting yourself in a little bit too deep here," Dillon said with a sigh. "You've only known her for a couple of weeks and already you've managed to get under her skin to the point where she is not speaking to you anymore." Dillon gave a little laugh. "It's obvious that she's still waiting for Travis to come, that she still loves him. I think you're putting yourself in harm's way, if you don't mind me saying."

"In harm's way? How?"

"At this moment in time, Gavin, you could just turn and walk away. Polly is not speaking to you, because you ran off at the mouth, so I think it's a perfect opportunity for you to save yourself. You don't need to get into this any deeper than you are already, because she is in love with somebody else. I reckon what I'm trying to say is that I think you're setting yourself up for a fall when there's no need. You can't be in love with her yet, and if you stay away from her, you might never be at all. There's plenty of other pretty girls in Oregon."

"There sure are, but none of them have managed to turn my head in all the time I've been here. One year and eight months and *nothing* until I saw her," Gavin said a little wistfully.

"There will be others," Dillon said firmly. "I promise you. Just give it a little time and I'm sure you will happen upon a young lady every bit as pretty and every bit as appealing as Polly Whitaker. Only next time, the young lady might have a free heart, not one chained to a man who is so far away he barely exists anymore."

"I'm not so sure."

"Why are you so drawn to her?"

"Because underneath all that determination to wait for a man that even *she* doesn't think is coming for her, there's a real bright and funny girl in there. Sure, she's pretty, real pretty. But that's not it, not all of it." Gavin paused for a moment and stared off across the great expanse of Goodman's merchant store. "There's just something about her that makes me want to make that sadness leave her beautiful brown eyes. I want to be the one to make her happy. That's as best as I know how to explain it." Gavin shrugged.

"Uh-oh!" Dillon said with a broad grin as he lightly slapped his own forehead.

"What do you mean? *What?*" Gavin said, feeling a little wrong-footed.

"It means forget everything I've just said. It's clear that you're already in deep enough. I thought you just had a liking for the girl, which would be sensible. But you're just diving right in with both feet, aren't you?"

"There's just something about her," Gavin repeated, hoping *that* was explanation enough.

"Well, I think I should just warn you, you may have a long wait."

"You mean I need to wait long enough for Polly to realize that Travis is never coming?"

"Yes, but not only that," Dillon said and patted the sack next to him, indicating that Gavin would do better to sit down for a while. "But then you'll have to wait a while longer for her to get over it. And then maybe even longer still for her to trust somebody again. Look, I think this Travis character was her first love. You know what the ladies are like with first loves, they take a good long while to get over it if they don't marry them."

"What do you know about him?" Gavin asked, and it was a question that he had wanted to ask for a long time.

Ever since he had met Polly, ever since he had spent those first few minutes knowing that she had grabbed his attention more than anybody else had done. Gavin had been keen to know the details of the man who seemed to be held so tightly inside her precious heart.

"He's about your age, maybe twenty-two or three." Dillon began with the obvious facts. "I guess you'd call him a handsome man. Well, you would if you were a young woman like Polly Whitaker." Dillon laughed.

"I guess I kind of figured that he'd be handsome." Gavin shrugged in a way which he hoped would convey a certain nonchalance. Nonchalance that he didn't really feel.

"I never heard him speaking of any family. But to be straight, I didn't really have a great deal to do with him. I remember him just being there more than anything else."

"So, you didn't get to know him?"

"No, but they were quite an obvious couple, I suppose."
Dillon paused for a moment, seemingly looking back to his
time on the Oregon Trail. "I mean, it was clear they'd met
there on the trail. They'd taken up with each other just a few
days into it and they were something of a regular feature
every night. You know, when the wagons circled at night, it
was immense. You can't imagine it, Gavin, coming across
with only a hundred or so." He squinted slightly and shook
his head as though in disbelief. "Coming across with over a
thousand, there were just so many wagons. We had music
and dancing every night, especially in the beginning. And
there weren't so many losses and everyone was excited, and I
think Polly and Travis were a big part of that. They were
young, they seemed to have fallen in love, and they spent
every night wandering around inside the wagon circle hand-
in-hand, or dancing, that sort of thing."

"No wonder she fell in love with him," Gavin said bleakly.

"I suppose people just gravitate towards one another in those
circumstances. I mean, I already had my eye on Trinity and
we might have been a little bit more like Polly and Travis,
you know, excited and what have you, if Trinity's father
hadn't died the way he did." Dillon shrugged.

"So, they only had eyes for each other then?"

"She only had eyes for him; that was for sure," Dillon said a
little cryptically.

"What do you mean?"

"I could be wrong, I mean, I had a lot going on with three
ladies to help out. Although it's true to say that they helped
me as much as I helped them." Dillon laughed. "Anyway, I
reckon I saw Travis' eye wandering here and there on
occasion. Nothing too obvious, nothing that Polly would

have seen. Just now and then in the daytime as we were all moving. I'd see him occasionally and, if Polly was helping her mama or daddy with something, Travis would have a good look about him. I was fairly sure at times that he was having a good look at some of the other young ladies going across that trail with their families."

"And Polly never knew?"

"I wasn't so sure of it myself. In fact, it was something that I had more or less forgotten about until Trinity and Polly became friends here in Oregon. They'd never particularly got to know each other in the wagon train, but you know what Trinity is like. She saw Polly in the store and that was that, friends for life." Dillon laughed.

"Your wife is certainly one of the good ones, Dillon. I hope you know how lucky you are."

"Every day, my friend, every day."

"So, what does Trinity think of it all?" Gavin asked, keen to get that smart woman's perspective without actually having to ask her himself.

"Well, when I mentioned to her that I was sure that I'd seen Travis' eye wander now and again back out on the trail all those months ago, she told me she'd seen very much the same thing herself. But she said she hadn't given it much thought. Trinity said that she always found something kind of lifting and inspiring about the way the two of them had met and fallen in love so quickly. I guess she didn't want to believe that one-half of the fairy-tale was maybe not quite as in love as he appeared to be. And then, of course, tragedy struck Trinity's own life, and she more or less stopped paying attention."

"That's understandable," Gavin sighed. "And to be honest, I'm inclined to think that if Trinity thought she saw something, then she really did. Not much gets past her, does it?"

"Nothing gets past her." Dillon threw his head back and laughed. "Nothing at all."

"I don't know if this is good news or bad," Gavin said, mulling it all over. "If this Travis has a wandering eye, I reckon it's a fair suggestion that he's set up with somebody else now down in California."

"From your point of view, I guess that would be the good news." Dillon shrugged.

"But once she comes to truly realize it herself, that's going to pull the stuffing right out of Polly, isn't it?" Gavin said and felt suddenly very low.

"And that bothers you a lot, doesn't it?" Dillon said quietly.

"I think that bothers me more than anything."

"Well then, you really *will* have to forget everything I said in the beginning." Dillon slowly shook his head from side to side. "Don't bother trying to forget her, because you're already halfway to being in love with that woman already. You'll just have to bide your time and be ready to wait. And I must admit, I've got a sneaking suspicion that you'll be able to do it without too much trouble."

## CHAPTER 5

"*P*olly, honey, that nice young man called to see you again, but I had to tell him that you were down in the town with Trinity," Angela Whitaker said as she busied herself cleaning the great cast-iron pot that she had used to make the family a stew that evening.

"Oh, did he?" Polly said in a noncommittal fashion.

Gavin had called around to her family's farmhouse more than once, and quite unexpectedly in the last weeks. Polly could sense that the time was coming to have some sort of conversation with her mama, but she still did not want to.

She couldn't help but wonder if her mother wasn't just a little bit relieved that some other man had taken an interest in her. Perhaps she, too, thought the worst of Travis Hurst and didn't believe that he was coming back for her either.

"Your daddy sure does like him. A real good farming man, seems like." Angela went on as if trying to coax her daughter into conversation.

"What difference does it make what he does for a living?" Polly snapped, although she knew she didn't have a right to.

After all, her mother was doing nothing wrong at all, just caring for her. Perhaps if she had discussed things with her mother all along, Angela would have had a better idea how her daughter was feeling. The fact that the poor woman had to cast about in the dark in hopes of discovering something was Polly's fault, and she knew it.

"I'm just making conversation, honey. Don't you go biting my head off," Angela said, and Polly was immediately apologetic.

"Oh, Mama, I'm so sorry." Polly dashed across the kitchen and threw herself into her mother's arms.

Angela, despite having wet hands from cleaning the pan, threw her arms around her daughter and held her tightly.

"Why don't you just tell me what's happening?" Angela said in soothing tones. "I don't know how to help you unless you speak to me."

"I'm sorry, Mama, it's all just so confusing."

"Feelings always are." Angela rubbed her daughters back and Polly could just feel the vague dampness from her wet hands.

"One minute I think Travis is never going to come back for me and I get so angry and upset with him I think I might never forgive him," Polly began, speaking from the heart. "And the next I think that he'll come for me; of course, he'll come for me. We love each other and I should trust him. And then, in those times, I feel guilty for betraying him."

"Now, how on earth are you betraying him?"

35

"Well, by thinking wrong of him," Polly began. "And for having other feelings," she said a little more cautiously.

"You mean feelings for Gavin Swain?" Angela asked gently

"I don't know." And it was true, Polly really couldn't pick through her feelings and make any sense of them.

GAVIN HAD BEGUN to drop by a few weeks before, just after he had upset her in Mrs. Taplow's diner. After she'd stormed out, Polly had assumed that their friendship had come to an end. And, as that particular day had worn on, she knew she was coming to regret it. She didn't like the idea that her new friendship was finished just because she'd lost her temper.

In fact, she had worried about it so much that she had hardly slept that night. By the time the day had rolled around to lunchtime, Polly had been shattered.

However, she came round pretty quickly when there came a loud knock at the back door of the house, the door that led into the kitchen. Knowing that her mother was down in the town having some tea and conversation with Mrs. Jeannie Stanton, Polly had hurried through the little sitting room and the kitchen to answer the door.

"I'm sorry," Gavin said and held his hands up in front of him, palms forward.

"Gavin? What are you doing here?" Polly said, surprised at how relieved she was to see him.

"I'm here to apologize, Polly. I know I made you angry yesterday and I don't want us to go falling out over it. I ran off at the mouth when I should have been quiet, and you had every right to leave me there with more pie and coffee than I could manage." When he got to the end of his little speech, Polly could see the corners of his mouth turning up.

"Oh, just come in," Polly said, laughing as she tugged at the sleeve of his checked shirt and pulled him into the kitchen. "And I wanted to apologize to you, anyway." She became a little more serious.

"You have nothing to apologize to me for. I was the one who spoke out of turn, not you." Gavin was serious also for a moment.

"Well, I guess you just spoke your mind. I didn't need to walk away from you."

"And you missed out on some truly wonderful pie, by the way." It was, as always, clear to see the mirth in Gavin's bright blue eyes.

"I suppose you ate the whole lot, did you?" Polly said, holding an arm out towards the kitchen table and indicating that he should take a seat.

"Sure did, it was wonderful." He grinned and patted his belly.

"So, you weren't so distressed at the idea of losing your new friend then?" For some reason, Polly felt a little crestfallen.

"Of course, I was." Gavin's voice was suddenly low and his lopsided grin all gone. "Mrs. Taplow wrapped the pie for me to take home. I had two sips of coffee and that was that."

"I'm sorry," Polly said with a great sigh. "I'm doing it again, aren't I?"

"I didn't want to drop the mood to a low point by telling you that I didn't want to eat the pie without you being there," Gavin said and then smiled. "But let's not fall out over pie,

Polly Whitaker. After all, I'm sure we can find many much more interesting things to fall out over instead."

"I'm sure we can," Polly said, thinking that she probably ran off at the mouth much more than Gavin did.

"So, are we friends again?"

"We sure are." Polly smiled and set about putting some coffee on the stove.

"In that case, is there any pie? I only ask because I haven't eaten since yesterday." He slumped sideways in his chair, playing dead. "I just haven't been able to face it." As his voice died away into a theatrical death scene, Polly threw her head back and laughed.

"There's a little apricot pie left, but I don't think you're going to be as pleased to see it as you would be if it was Mrs. Taplow's," Polly said with a wince, knowing exactly how dry her mother's pastry was.

"I'm not a fussy man. I only get pie if I go down into the town and buy it, I'm useless at cooking anything. So I'm just quietly pleased for anything that comes my way."

"I never know when to take you seriously," Polly said, doubtfully cutting him a slice of the pie.

"I suppose it is a bit of a problem," Gavin said and drummed his fingers on the table. "Maybe I should give you a sign or something if I'm going to say something serious?" He went on and Polly laughed. "Maybe I could just tell you that what I'm about to say serious, and then follow it up with something, well, *serious*."

"Just eat your pie," Polly said as she placed the plate down in front of him.

Gavin had called a couple of times a week since then, and every visit seemed to be full of fun, even if her mother was around. And once, Gavin had called when her father was there and the two of them had got along just fine.

"POLLY, there's nothing wrong in having feelings for Gavin, if you really have them," her mother spoke finally and released her from her soggy grip.

"It just all seems so complicated."

"Because of Travis?" It was the first time in a long time that Angela had mentioned Travis.

"Yes, because of Travis," Polly said and felt suddenly miserable. "I really did think that he would come back for me, Mama."

"Oh, come here," Angela said, scooping her daughter back into her arms once more. "Sometimes men get carried away, and sometimes they don't keep their promises. But just because one man doesn't keep a promise, doesn't mean that another man will do the same. I know Travis was your first love, Polly, and I know how hard it can be to let go of, believe me."

"How do you know? Did you love somebody before Daddy?"

"I sure did," Angela said with a chuckle. "Or at least I thought I did, I think that's the truth."

"But how did you make yourself love again? I mean, I know you love Daddy."

"You don't have to *make* yourself love again, sweetheart. It just happens. Love just happens, and there's not a thing you can do about it when it comes." She smiled and stared off a little into the distance as if remembering the moment at which she had fallen in love with Clarence Whitaker. "The heart will do, what the heart wants to do. And there's nothing you can do to stop it."

"Well, I just don't know what to do next," Polly sighed.

"You don't have to do anything, do you?"

"I suppose not, but I can't help feeling like I'm supposed to be making a decision of some sort."

"Why? Has Gavin asked you? Is he insisting that you choose one way or the other?"

"No, he's never mentioned anything about it. I told him that we could only be friends, and he was happy with that, and he's never gone against it, not really."

"But Polly, he turns up here in this kitchen twice a week and he finds you in town every time you go. That man might be content to be your friend forever, but don't doubt that he loves you, honey, because he does. I never saw a man so head over heels as Gavin," Angela chuckled.

"But what about Travis? Surely you must have seen *him* head over heels as well?" Polly said and felt a little dismayed.

"I'm sure he cared for you a good deal, sweetheart. He was a very nice young man," Angela spoke without a lot of conviction.

"You don't believe that for a minute, Mama, do you?"

"Polly, don't you go getting all snippy with me again." Angela laughed. "I'm just trying to help, remember?"

"I don't mean to be snippy, Mama, it just hurts to think that Travis didn't feel for me what I feel for him."

"But do you *still* feel that way about him, Polly, or is it just habit? Is it just pride and bruised feelings, or do you really *love* Travis?"

POLLY HAD BEEN unable to answer and, for several days after, could come to no real conclusion. But even though she could not fully describe to herself her own feelings for Travis, she was a little more certain of the feelings she had for Gavin.

She knew that she looked forward to his visits to their home, and hoped that every time she went into town he would be there somewhere, lurking and waiting for her to appear.

His curious handsomeness had grown on her with every day that passed, as did his carefree sense of humor and good company. All in all, Polly was starting to think of Gavin more and more. Even though she tried to stop herself, even though she would try to combat it with thoughts of Travis, still Gavin had managed to worm his way into her heart and mind, just a little more.

## CHAPTER 6

The following morning, Polly was glad that she had, in the end, opened up to her mother just a little. Although they had not managed to solve her problem between them during their conversation, just the fact that they had talked about it seemed to have cleared her mind a good deal.

Polly had put some thought into the idea of first love and how it could affect a person. When she thought about it, she realized that she had perhaps clung onto the idea of Travis more than anything, because she couldn't believe that something as intense as that first love could ever be replaced.

Maybe she had tortured herself with constant thoughts of all the good things; the excitement of the wagon train and a new life and her first love with a very handsome man. Dancing in the circled wagons at night and the moments shared alone when it seemed that everybody else was preoccupied preparing food.

Polly remembered, above all things, a very general feeling.

Surely, it wasn't all about Travis, but everything that she had felt then, every excitement, not just the romance.

And if it was a romance that she really wanted, she had the offer of it right there in Oregon. And not a second-best or a consolation prize, but a good and handsome man.

Polly felt suddenly lighter in her heart than she had done for a long time. It felt good to admit to herself that Travis really wasn't going to come for her after all and it felt better still to determine that it was time to get on with her own life. Maybe she would even tell Gavin a little bit about it.

She began to hum to herself as she got ready to set off for her usual run into town for their provisions, when there came a loud knock at the door.

Polly almost laughed out loud, thinking that it must surely be Gavin. If it was, he certainly had his days all mixed up. He already knew her routine off by heart but would seem to have forgotten that she would be heading into town that day. He usually found her there.

With a laugh, she made her way to the door and opened it wide. For a moment, her smile was frozen on her lips as she realized she was looking at none other than Travis Hurst.

"Travis?" She said, her breath coming in ragged gasps.

"Hey, Polly," he said and smiled at her, holding out both arms.

However, Polly didn't simply walk into them, she couldn't. She stood rooted to the spot staring at him, her body a mixture of numb and tingling with the shock of seeing him standing there.

After a moment, when it was clear that she was not about to fling herself into his arms, Travis let them drop to his side a little self-consciously. It was the first time she had ever seen him even vaguely self-conscious.

"Polly, you look good enough to eat," Travis said, his smile broad and every bit as handsome as she remembered it. "I sure have missed you."

"I can't believe that you're here," Polly said, it was the truth.

For all that she had imagined their wonderful meeting when they were finally reunited, she had never imagined the curious feeling she had at that moment. It was like being in a strange kind of limbo and she didn't know what to do or say for the best. She certainly didn't feel like throwing her arms around him before hastily packing a bag to leave for California.

"Aren't you going to ask me in?" Travis asked, making a move to step inside.

"Of course, come in, Travis." As Polly pushed the door closed behind him, she realized that her hands were shaking.

She wanted to distract herself for a while with coffee making or something similar, but wasn't sure that she could trust her shaking hands to see her through it.

"I sure have missed you," Travis said again, and looked at her hopefully. "Honey, please tell me that nothing's changed. You seem so different."

Again, Polly didn't know what to say. She knew she should be telling him how much she had missed him too. After all, it was nothing other than the absolute truth. And yet she couldn't quite say it, not then. Maybe it was the shock, but maybe it was simply that she had waited so long for him to come for her that her emotions had been beaten down until they were as flat as pancakes.

"No, it's the same old me," she said, but only because she knew she must say something.

"Is everything alright, Polly? I mean, is everything alright with your mama and daddy? They're both well?" Travis looked concerned, as if thinking some tragedy or other must surely account for her curious reception of him.

"Mama and Daddy are just fine, Travis." She smiled. "They're both out on the farm at the moment. In fact, I was just about to head into town. It's my day for collecting our provisions." Polly knew how weak that sounded and yet, for some reason, she would have given anything for him to simply release her so that she could ride the cart into town and clear her head.

The fact that Travis was there, at that moment, standing in her kitchen seemed somehow too much. She was about to be overwhelmed with all sorts of emotions; emotions that she couldn't rightly name. And the truth was that she didn't want to act on any of them until she knew exactly what they were.

"Thank God for that," Travis said and let out a great sigh. "And you, everything is alright with you?" He seemed as if he wanted to take a step towards her but did not.

The result was that they simply stood in the kitchen, some six feet between them, staring at each other.

"Yes, yes, I'm perfectly alright," she said, although faltering. "Really."

"You seemed so different," Travis said and she could see in his eyes that he was confused.

"I'm sorry, I guess I'm just surprised to see you."

"Surprised? But why?" Travis looked a little affronted.

"When I didn't hear from you, I was so worried," she said

quietly. "And the longer it went on, the more I came to think that you weren't coming for me at all. It's been ten months, Travis, since I arrived here in Oregon. And it's been almost a year since I last saw you, since you left me at the Parting of the Ways."

THE FORK in the trail commonly known as the Parting of the Ways was a place that Polly knew she would never forget as long as she lived. It was the place in which she had experienced her first jolt of searing pain and heartbreak, and it was a feeling that she hoped never to experience again for as long as she lived.

For the preceding months, Polly had almost convinced herself that, when the time came, Travis just wouldn't be able to take that fork in the road, to head south towards California without her. She had been slowly trying to persuade him to turn his hand to farming, or to become a ranch-hand or something similar. He was a big strong man and she felt certain that he could have turned his hand to anything he chose.

But there, on that last day when the wagon train stopped only long enough for those who were heading south to come out of the great line and bid farewell to the friends they had made along the way, she knew that all her cajoling and persuading had been in vain.

"Please, please, Travis. Don't leave me, there'll be all sorts of work in Oregon that you can do, I just know it."

"Honey, I'm just not cut out to be a farmer," he said with a shrug. "No, gold mining is for me."

"Then take me with you," Polly said hurriedly. "There's a

minister here, we'll get him to marry us this minute, and then we can head off to California together as man and wife."

"No, there's no sense in rushing this," Travis said, and Polly felt her heart begin to break.

"Rushing?" she said, with tears rolling down her cheeks.

"That's it, rushing," Travis said a little more firmly than she would have liked. "There's no sense in us rushing into it. I don't want you to have to get married at the side of the wagon train and head off into a future that isn't yet settled. I want to do this right. I want to get some money by me and come back to you. Without that, I don't have anything to offer you, Polly. I love you, but there's only one way to do this is, and that's the right way."

"You have everything I want *now*. I could come with you and we could find that life together," Polly said, desperately hanging onto his arm. "Please, Travis. Please don't leave me."

"I'm not leaving you, I'm just going to get our life all set up. I'll be back over to Oregon to get you before you know it." He smiled reassuringly and kissed her.

"Well, you see that you write me as soon as you get to California. You just send me a letter every day to the mail office in Oregon and I will count the days until I see you again."

"You can count on it. As *soon* as I get there."


Polly stepped backward across the kitchen as if trying to get away from the memory of it all.

"Polly?"

"I'm going to make some coffee," she said flatly.

"Polly, what did you mean *when you didn't hear from me?* Are you saying that you didn't get any of my letters?"

"Travis, I didn't get a single letter from you," Polly said, her voice dry and raspy. "Up until very recently, I went to that mail office every day, just as I told you I would. But no, there was never anything there for me. In the end, I just made a fool of myself."

"Are you sure you went to the right mail office?"

"This town is not so big yet that it has more than one," Polly said dismissively and then turned her back on him to begin to make coffee.

Her hands had stopped shaking, finally, but she still had the feeling that she wanted some distraction. For, as sad and as desolate as she had been those last months, this was the first time that she had felt genuinely angry with him. Maybe it was because he was safe and well, which meant that she was safe now to let her anger flow.

"Well, I sent them, Polly. Not every day, not as many as I would have liked, but several a week." Travis looked curiously devastated. "I wish I had sent them *every* day, but I was just working so hard."

"Oh yes, the goldmines," Polly said, and she felt as if she were in a strange dream that she couldn't get out of, couldn't wake up from.

"Well, I *did* work the gold mines."

"And now you're here," Polly said, slamming the pan down onto the stove angrily.

"Polly, please don't," Travis said and was suddenly behind

her, his arms around her. "I love you and I don't know what happened to those letters, but I swear to you that I sent them. In the end, when I didn't get a reply from you, I thought you'd decided against me. But I had to know, you see. I had to see you with my own eyes and hear you turn me away your way with your own voice."

"Oh, Travis," Polly said, hardly knowing how she felt.

"Don't turn me away, Polly, please."

## CHAPTER 7

"So, how long is Travis in town?" Dillon asked as the two of them leaned up against the fencing at the back of the merchant store in the cool autumn air.

"To be honest, I don't know. I don't think Polly knows either. Actually, I didn't even ask, perhaps I should have," Gavin said, realizing that he had missed a crucial opportunity to find out if Travis intended to stay in town.

"Well, if he's keeping to his job on the barges, I can't think he'll be here for long," Dillon said with a hopeful shrug.

"That's if he intends to keep that job. I guess it's hard to say with this guy. One minute he's digging for gold, the next minute he's working on the Willamette River."

"And how long has he been working on the barges?"

"Just a month or so, according to Polly. She said as soon as he got tipped out of the goldmine he was working at, he went straight for the barges."

"But why? I mean, gold mining is surely a better job than

being on the barges, traveling up and down the river and never settling."

"I'd have thought so too," Gavin said thoughtfully. "But I didn't like to mention it to Polly. I've already made a mistake once of suggesting that Travis isn't to be trusted. I don't want to run the risk of her turning away from me again."

"But Gavin, now that Travis is here, don't you run the risk of losing her anyway?" Dillon winced. "I know it's harsh, my friend, but it's true. I don't think you've got anything to lose by pointing out one or two things to her."

"But what? After all, he just might not have taken to the gold mining."

"Is that what he told her?" Dillon asked skeptically.

"No, he told her that the mining manager had taken a dislike to him and made things real tough for him down there. In the end, he decided to move on. That was when he made his way to the Willamette and got a start on the cargo barges."

"And sailed all the way up here to find his true love, huh?" Dillon still sounded skeptical.

"That's more or less as she told it to me, yes."

"And is that it? Are they actually together again? Trinity can't get to the bottom of it at all, she can't pin Polly down to a firm answer, and she knows it isn't really her place to keep pushing."

"I guess it's not my place either," Gavin said sadly.

"Maybe it *is* your place." Dillon ventured. "I mean, these last weeks, I thought the two of you were starting to get real close."

"And we were, I know it. Even the other day…" Gavin couldn't finish.

HE'D SEEN POLLY in the town and they had spent more than an hour in Mrs. Taplow's diner in deep conversation.

As Polly had told him every detail of Travis' sudden appearance, Gavin had felt his heart sink lower than his boots. However, Polly didn't speak of Travis with the excitement that he had somehow imagined she would. Instead, she seemed exhausted and uncertain and, despite the fact that he did not like to see her so out of sorts, Gavin had to admit, that it gave him the thinnest sliver of hope.

"Polly, I know I promised to be nothing more than your friend, but it was an easy promise to make when I thought there was still hope for me," Gavin began and Polly stared at him miserably. "But I want to retract that now."

"You want to retract your friendship?" Polly said, and looked suddenly desolate.

"No, I don't want to retract my friendship." Gavin reached out and tentatively laid his hand on top of hers. "I want to retract my promise not to try for anything more than friendship. You must know how I feel about you, Polly. And trust me, I wouldn't have said anything about it, I wouldn't have pushed. I was happy to wait to see how things worked out between us, or even *if* they worked out between us. Now I feel as if I've lost you before we've even begun, just because Travis has sailed up the river into town."

"You always knew about Travis, Gavin. And I told you that he'd come for me, didn't I?"

"You did, I know you did." Gavin didn't know what else to say.

"And I know that you know I had doubts about it myself, because I did. Big doubts. But he's here now."

"And is he here to stay?" Gavin asked, although he felt certain that she wouldn't entirely welcome his questions. "Is he going to settle here in town now that he doesn't have work in California anymore?"

"I don't know yet, Gavin."

Polly looked exhausted, and he felt guilty for pressing her.

"Nothing seems real at the moment, Gavin. I can't really tell you how it is that I feel since Travis has come back to me because, honestly, I don't know. I think I need time to get used to it, to get over the shock of it all, before I can really think about how I feel. I just need a little time; time to think."

Gavin hadn't seen her for some days afterward and, by the time he was in conversation with his friend over it, he felt much more *lost at sea,* than he appeared.

"I don't know, Dillon," Gavin said on the wave of a long drawn-out sigh. "I guess the time has come for me to give up."

"Give up?" Dillon sounded surprised.

"You know what, I really *should* have taken your advice when you'd first given it. You told me back then that I was setting myself up, that there had been time for me to walk away before my feelings ran too deep. Foolishly, I didn't take that advice."

"I think the advice was redundant already by the time I gave it, Gavin. Don't be so hard on yourself."

"Maybe, Dillon, but I think that it's time that I took that advice now, however much I don't want to."

"Well, I hate to confuse things for you, Gavin, but I no longer agree with the advice I gave you back then," Dillon said and chuckled.

"Why? What do you mean?"

"There's just something about this whole Travis situation that doesn't add up," Dillon said. "For one thing, that whole business of none of his letters arriving doesn't hold water, does it?"

"No, I don't suppose it does."

"I mean, not *every* single letter sent from the mail office down there to the mail office up here can have gone astray, can it?"

"Unless he was handing the letters to somebody else to take to the mail office and they never took them?" Gavin said, although he didn't think much of his own explanation.

"I think that's pretty unlikely, don't you? And if it had been the case, Travis would have been better off telling her that. After all, it would explain things better than simply saying his letters had gone astray."

"In the end, it doesn't matter, does it? The only thing that matters is the fact that Polly seems to have accepted the explanation. I know that neither you nor I believe it, and probably Trinity doesn't either, but we are not in Polly's shoes, are we? In the end, it's only her opinion of the thing that matters, isn't it? She's the only one who's got to choose."

"Alright, but just hear me out," Dillon said somewhat forcefully. "Because it's not just the idea of the letters that sets a bug of suspicion running up and down my back. I sat down the other night and had a good long talk with Trinity. I asked her everything that Polly's told her over the months about her and Travis."

"And?" Gavin said, suddenly a little more interested.

"Well, we talked it back and forth and there was just something that didn't sit right with either one of us."

"What was that?"

"Why didn't he marry her at the time?" Dillon said and spread his arms wide.

"I think I've already said this to *you*, haven't I?" Gavin said, somewhat confused.

"I know you have, and I know I wasn't really paying proper attention at the time. But it's right, isn't it? Everyone setting off on the Oregon Trail didn't really know what was ahead of them, did they? I mean, Travis Hurst wasn't the only one, was he? And so, when he finds a woman who is willing to marry him, no matter what the future holds, why wouldn't he just take her with him?" Dillon paused for a moment as if trying to add to his point. "Polly told Trinity of their last moments at the Parting of the Ways, and how she begged him to marry her there and then, to take her with him. And he was, apparently, so determined to make some money, to have a place of his own before they could settle down, that he wouldn't hear of it. And now, when he no longer even works at the mine and seems to have a tenuous job on the barges, he suddenly wants her. It doesn't make sense, does it?"

"No, you're right, it doesn't."

"So, I'm just gonna say it right out, Gavin," Dillon said after taking a deep breath. "I think he ducked out on her that day at the Parting of the Ways. It is my honest belief, now I come to think about it all, he just didn't want to take her with him. She kept him company all the way along the Oregon Trail, kept him diverted, added a little excitement to his day. But when California beckoned, with new excitement and opportunities, I think he just turned his back on her with nothing more than a promise that he would write. I think he's a dog, Gavin, and Polly deserves better."

"And is that what Trinity thinks too?" Gavin asked, as if he needed Trinity's seal of approval on Dillon's musings.

"That is *exactly* what Trinity thinks. I think she thought it for a long while but didn't want to say it out loud. After all, no girl wants to hear that, do they? No girl wants to think that she was just a distraction on a long journey and nothing more."

"But why would he come back for her now? What's changed in Travis's life that has made Polly a prospect for him at last?" Gavin said, almost to himself.

"Exactly, my friend," Dillon said, smiling happily as if relieved his friend had finally caught on to his line of thinking.

"Well, without actually setting off for California, I don't know how we'll ever get to the bottom of it." Gavin's enthusiasm had turned instantly into dejection again.

"Oh, I'm sure there'll be somebody on one of those barges who knows a thing or two about Travis Hurst," Dillon said knowingly. "After all, a big blond man like that, a guy who looks like a Viking next to everybody else, stands out, doesn't he? There's bound to be somebody down on the barges who knows something about him. It doesn't even have to be the barge he's on, a lot of those barges are run by just a few going concerns."

"So, you think I should ask around?" Gavin asked doubtfully.

"Why not?" Dillon said and clapped a hand hard on his back. "Just don't give up, Gavin. You have one thing left to try and I think you should do it. If you don't at least give it a shot, I think you'll live to regret it. I know that she might end up trundling off into the sunset with Travis, whatever you do, I'm not going to lie to you. But if she does, at least you'll know you did everything in your power to keep her. And if there's something to be known about Travis Hurst, however painful it might be, Polly deserves to know it."

## CHAPTER 8

"So, he's going? He's leaving town?" Gavin asked as he and Polly walked slowly around the edge of one of her father's immense fields.

Gavin had called around, and she had been relieved that Travis was at work down on the river. She didn't want to have to explain Gavin's presence, since she had talked of him very little. Certainly, she had given Travis the impression that they were nothing more than vague acquaintances, two people who had met through mutual friends. And of course, in the end, that's what they had been. Not casual acquaintances, but certainly not anything more than friends, whatever she had come to feel for him.

"He has to. He's moving onto a shorter cargo run, a more regular one, near Portland. He is looking to settle down up there instead."

"So, Travis is going to keep hold of this job on the barges, is he?"

"Gavin, please don't say it like that," Polly said, and felt suddenly defensive. "It's not as if Travis didn't try his hardest. If you work somewhere, in a mine, and the manager takes a dislike to you, there's nothing you can do about it. Travis worked hard, the mine manager just didn't like him and that's all there was to it. He knew he wouldn't get a start anywhere else in the area, so he didn't have much of a choice."

"I'm not sure that losing your position in one mine means that you can't work in any of the neighboring ones, Polly."

"Gavin, if you've come here to make trouble for me, then I'd rather you just go," Polly said, although she wasn't entirely sure that she *did* want him to go.

She'd been purposely keeping away from him in the days since Travis had returned because she knew that her feelings for Gavin were complicating everything. She still hadn't settled back into her old feelings for Travis, and she felt certain that Gavin was the cause of it. On that day, that very morning before Travis had arrived at her door, Polly knew that she had been about to open up to her own feelings for Gavin and not only that, but she had planned to let him know about it. She had wanted him to become more than just a friend. And, had Travis not appeared, she felt sure that she and Gavin would now be together, not only together, but happy.

"Don't do that again, Polly," Gavin said in a level tone. "Don't send me away again, or walk away from me just because I said the wrong thing."

"I'm sorry."

"It was hard enough the first time, and that was back when my feelings hadn't had the chance to develop into what they are now. If I am trying to get you to look at things a little

59

more closely, can't you see it's because I don't want to lose you? Can't you see that I want you to at least think about it before you turn and walk away from me forever? Please, Polly, just look at it, look at it closely."

"Look at what? What is there to look at?" Polly could feel herself getting angry but she knew, in her heart of hearts, it was because there was certainly something in what Gavin was saying, but she was still trying to hide from the truth.

There was plenty to look at, plenty to study at close quarters and mull over thoroughly. And yet, for some reason, she had been afraid to do it. She kept feeling the awful pain she had felt at the Parting of the Ways and knew that she didn't want to risk feeling it again. If she pressed Travis too hard, if she asked for too many explanations, wouldn't she just push him away? And if he walked away from her now, how would she feel? In truth, she didn't actually know, she didn't want to look at it.

All Polly knew was that she didn't want to have her heart torn out afresh; she couldn't risk it.

"I think you know as well as I do, there's plenty to look at, Polly." Gavin went on relentlessly. "For one thing, do you really accept his explanation of why you never received a single letter from him? Do you really believe that deep down?"

"Gavin, anything could have happened to those letters."

"Yes, there's an outside chance that one of them might have made its way through and actually been delivered. And that's my point, really. For *some* of them to go astray is perfectly possible, but all of them? I know the mail isn't perfect, but it's not as bad as all that."

"Gavin, Travis is real sincere about it. He even said that he had to come here to see me with his own eyes because he thought I wasn't replying to his letters."

"I can see that I'm not going to get anywhere with this, am I? You've already decided to believe him, whether you truthfully believe him or not. And you know, that's what worries me more than anything, Polly. You're so determined to believe him, every word of what he says. I think it's blinding you to the man himself."

"And what do *you* know of Travis Hurst? You've never even met the man. You've never had two minute's conversation with him, so how can you say that I'm blind to him? How can you know there's anything to be blind to?"

"Polly Whitaker, I never knew a woman as quick to temper as you," Gavin said and suddenly he was grinning at her. "I keep getting the feeling that any minute I'm going to have to duck."

"Gavin!" Polly said, and found that she was laughing for the first time in days.

Oh, how she'd missed their time together; how she'd missed the way he had of finding something funny in every situation. And how grateful she was of it at that moment when she had felt nothing but fear and confusion for many days.

"I think I'll just put a bit of space between us to be on the safe side," Gavin said, and took two paces sideways away from her as they continued to walk slowly around the edge of the field.

"You know, you're real silly at times," Polly said, and continued to laugh.

"See what you'd be missing if you went away to live in Portland? Who'd make you laugh then, that's what I want to know?"

"I didn't say I was going to Portland."

"And you didn't say you weren't going either." Gavin looked serious again.

"I just don't know," she said, and meant it.

Polly had never felt so torn in all her life. She hadn't meant to fall for Gavin, but she knew with all certainty that she had. But she had put such a block on her feelings for him in the last days that she didn't know if what she felt for him was enough. And, of course, as much as she didn't want to investigate her own feelings for Travis, she didn't want to investigate her feelings for Gavin either.

As far as Polly could see, if she let her feelings truly take a hold of her as she had done on the Oregon Trail, she couldn't make a move in either direction without having her heart broken.

She risked Travis walking away and the resurgence of the old pain, and she equally risked walking away from Gavin and finding a whole new pain would take its place. She truly did not know what to do for the best.

"Do you love him?" Gavin asked, quite out of the blue.

"I... I..."

"It shouldn't be a difficult question to answer. If you love someone, you love them flat out, no stuttering."

"You don't understand, Gavin," Polly said and wished that she could even begin to explain it to him.

The problem was, she knew that Gavin's own heart was heavily invested and he couldn't possibly remain impartial; he couldn't possibly just act as a friend and nothing more as she tried to explain the quandary she was in.

"Then help me to understand, Polly. Don't just leave me hanging here in limbo like this."

Gavin had closed the distance he had comically put between them until he was so close there was hardly space for a breath.

"Gavin, I can't explain it."

"More than anything, I want to ask you if you love me, Polly." Gavin held up a hand as if to silence her. "No, I don't want to hear your answer. I don't want to hear you stutter in confusion. But I still want to ask. Crazy, isn't it?"

"Gavin, if I'd realized at the time how much hurt was coming, I would never have gone to that barn dance."

Gavin's mouth dropped open and the look of horror on his face said it all. "You wish you'd never met me?"

"Oh God, no, I didn't mean that." Finally, tears began to roll down her cheeks.

In many ways, she wished that they *had* never met, it would make her decision so much simpler now. But she couldn't begin to imagine her life without Gavin in it. She thought of all the times he'd turned up in her mama's kitchen out of the blue with a mischievous grin on his face. She thought of how he'd made her laugh time and time again, and the faces he'd pulled as he tried to choke down the dry pastry of her mother's fruit pies.

She'd never met anybody like Gavin Swain in her life and she expected she never would again.

"Of course, I don't wish I'd never met you, Gavin. I can't get my meaning out just perfect at the moment, it's too hard. Please don't put words in my mouth, don't give meaning to every word I say because I am just so tired. I'm tired of trying to think in a straight line and come to a conclusion. It's just not coming to me the way it should."

"I'm sorry," Gavin said, and she could hear a little thickness in his voice which she knew was emotion. "I shouldn't have pushed, I shouldn't have said that." And with that, he just pulled her tight against his chest and wrapped his strong arms around her.

He held her tightly for what felt like minutes, neither one of them speaking. Everything about being in Gavin's arms felt right, just as she had felt all those months ago in Travis's arms. But she didn't want to compare them, not then. She wanted to just be there in that moment, not in the past and not in the future. She wanted the maelstrom of thoughts to simply dissolve into nothing, into a comforting darkness.

In the end, Polly couldn't have said how long the two of them stood there out on that field on a cold autumn afternoon in the pale sunshine, locked in each other's arms. As they slowly broke their embrace, Gavin's eyes held her own firmly and she felt sure, for a wonderful and terrible moment, that he was going to kiss her.

Polly knew that she wanted that kiss more than anything, and yet she *didn't* want it. She knew that it would bring yet more confusion, would cloud her mind and tear at her heart. In the last moment, she drew away from him and looked down at her feet.

## CHAPTER 9

"Just tell her what you found out, Gavin," Dillon said vehemently.

"When I first set out to find information, I thought it would be as simple as just telling her. Now that I know all there is to know about Hurst, it really isn't that simple," Gavin said.

"Why not?" Trinity said gently, and Gavin appreciated her tone.

"Because she is so confused already. And you can see to look at her that she is exhausted just thinking about it all."

"But won't this new information make things clearer for her?" Dillon sat down at the kitchen table and lifted one of the three coffee mugs his wife had just placed down.

"To be honest, I'm not sure it will. I think it would just upset her so much and I just don't want to do that to her."

"If you don't tell her, Polly could end up making the worst

decision of her life." Dillon took a sip of his scalding coffee and winced. "Ouch."

Gavin thought about that for a moment, thought about everything that he had found out about Travis. Dillon was right, of course. There was so much more to it than that.

When Gavin had first stumbled across the information, his first thought had been to hasten around to the Whitaker farmhouse and tell her everything there and then. In fact, he'd set off from the saloon bar in town and had walked some distance before he realized that he couldn't do it.

Not only did he not want to go into Polly's home smelling of drink, but he didn't want to bombard her with every painful detail.

On Dillon's advice, Gavin had made his way down to the Willamette River and hovered about in hopes of finding somebody, either on the same barge as Travis, or one of the others, who might be able to give him a bit more detail of the man.

It had all seemed so simple at first, a brilliant plan. But Gavin had stuck out like a sore thumb down at the Riverside amongst men lugging great sacks and moving to and fro, loading things onto carts from the boats, and vice versa. All in all, it was a hive of activity and he was the only man present not moving.

In the end, it began to draw attention, but not exactly the attention he wanted. He could see that the barge workers began to view him with a certain amount of suspicion and he knew that if he hovered for much longer one of them would certainly confront him.

And if he then asked for any available information on Travis, that would also be viewed with suspicion. And not only that, but the fact that a stranger had been down to the barges to ask about Travis would spread like wildfire and undoubtedly reach the ears of the man himself.

Feeling dejected, Gavin made his way through the cool late afternoon air back towards town. Whatever there was to find out about Travis Hurst, he felt sure that he would never hear of it. He'd failed, and he could hardly see how he could have ever succeeded after that fiasco.

There was only one thing that he knew for certain, and that was that he loved Polly. He'd fallen for her on their first meeting, intrigued by her initial standoffish manner and her scowling, and then beguiled by her frankness and humor.

Gavin found himself wandering into the saloon bar almost without realizing it. He sauntered in sadly thinking of Polly's dark golden hair and deep brown eyes and her beautiful face and wondering if he really was about to lose her forever. At that moment, he would have settled to be her friend for the rest of their lives, a friend and nothing more, if only she would stay.

"Beer?" The sullen bartender spoke as soon as Gavin took a stool at the bar.

"Please," he said and nodded.

The first drink barely touched the sides and yet it seemed to have done nothing to soothe the ache in his chest.

"Another?" The bartender said with a knowing look. He'd obviously seen it all before.

"Please," Gavin said again, feeling monosyllabic.

As Gavin tried to forget his failure down by the barges, he began to listen in to conversations all around him.

"I'm going to head back now, Jim," said a gruff voice just behind him. "And if you've got any sense, you'll be heading back now too. If you turn up back at the barge three sheets to the wind, the boss is going to have your hide."

"You worry too much," came another voice, which was undoubtedly Jim.

"Be it on your own head, Jim. But it's not the first time, is it? I don't think you can keep pushing the boss like this without finding yourself out of a position. But that's for you to worry about, I'm off now."

"Give me another beer, bartender," Jim spoke again and Gavin was aware of the man trying to pull himself up onto the bar stool at his side.

"And another one for me, when you're ready," Gavin added.

"This is good beer," Jim said, trying to strike up a conversation with Gavin.

"Maybe it's a bit too good," Gavin said with a smile as he wondered if he might have finally struck lucky.

"That sure is what my pal would say," Jim laughed.

"I guess he's just worried about you getting back to the barge in one piece." Gavin was keen to turn the conversation to Jim's working life.

"I guess so. He's one of the good ones."

"So, you in town for long?"

"Just a couple more days now. Then we're heading off up to Portland."

"Good life on the barges, is it?"

"It suits me. I don't particularly call anywhere home and I get to sleep on the barge so I'm happy."

"Is that the case for everybody who works on the barges?" Gavin wanted to appear interested without appearing to pry.

"No, the ones who get on a regular route tend to stay in one place. Set up home there, at one end of the route or the other, you know."

"Oh yes, I know of one of the barge workers who's just got himself a regular route and is thinking of setting up in Portland."

"Is that so?"

"Sure is. Travis something or other," Gavin said, trying not to appear too eager. "Hurt or Hurst or something?"

"There's only one Travis," Jim said with a snort.

"You know him?"

"Kind of," Jim spoke a little cautiously. "Friend of yours, is he?" Jim went on, and Gavin tried to gauge the man's mood by the look on his face.

Seeing that Jim seemed a little disapproving, Gavin thought he would hedge his bets.

"Not my kind of person, no," Gavin added a little shrug in the hope of appearing nonchalant.

"Not anybody's kind of person," Jim snorted again. "Although the ladies seem to like him. God knows why."

"Bit of a womanizer, is he?" Gavin chuckled and hoped that Jim was in the mood to gossip.

"Well, he's a mountain of a man with that bright blonde hair that the ladies seem to like. I reckon there's girls crying their eyes out about that man up and down the Willamette River."

"Really?" Gavin said, suddenly unable to believe his luck. "He's worked on the river long, has he?"

"Couple of months, I guess." Jim shrugged. "But one of the guys on another barge knew of him from California. Set himself up as a gold miner for a while."

"Just a while?"

"Yeah, got himself into a bit of trouble with the mine manager." Jim chuckled in a kind of merciless way.

"How so?" Gavin asked, and then looked at the bartender. "Two more beers, please."

"Decent of you." Jim nodded and reached out for his fresh beer. "Yeah, he got himself all nice and settled down with the mine manager's daughter by all accounts, merely days from getting hitched up. But that eye of his just kept roaming, he couldn't help himself. In the end, the manager's daughter broke their engagement, and I can't say I blame her."

"I guess her daddy wasn't too pleased either," Gavin said with a laugh.

"He tipped him out of the mine on the same day, and I reckon he made sure that Travis wouldn't get a start at any other mine for several miles across. By all accounts, that woman's daddy was not at all pleased at the way Hursty treated his little girl."

"What father would be?" Gavin felt that he had finally got something he really could take to Polly. "So, he headed straight for the barges then?" he went on.

"Sure did." Jim took a deep swig of his beer. "And is still up to his old tricks. I reckon he's got a girl everywhere we land of the river, and no mistake. He's even got one near, and we've only been moored up a week."

"Has he really?" Gavin felt a twinge, knowing that Jim was undoubtedly talking about Polly.

"Sure has. Reckons he's going to get himself set up with this one too, take her upriver to Portland, and marry her."

"That doesn't seem to fit well with his wandering eye." Gavin's mouth was dry and the beer suddenly tasted sour.

"Well, he'll stick to the river and carry on with his own little antics, I daresay. Best of both worlds, huh?" Jim raised his glass at his new friend and chuckled before taking another deep draft.

By the time Gavin had convinced himself that he really couldn't go to Polly with his new-found information, he began to wonder if everything had been in vain.


"DILLON IS RIGHT, Gavin. Polly really could be about to make a terrible mistake," Trinity's voice brought him back into the here and now.

"The more I think about it, the more I know that Polly already knows what sort of man Travis is. She might be avoiding the issue, but she knows. She is a smart woman and she's known it all along, right from the time when I first met her at the barn dance. Polly knew that he wasn't coming for her, I'm pretty sure she was certain of it. His arrival has certainly complicated things, but I don't think for a minute that she believes all that he's told her. I think we have to trust

71

Polly to make the right decision," Gavin said, and hoped that that would be an end to it.

"Gavin, I think there's something else you're not saying," Trinity said, almost apologetically.

"As always, you see right into the middle of things, don't you?" Gavin smiled warmly at Trinity. "You're quite right, there is something I'm not saying. And the reason I'm not saying it is because it makes me sound like the most selfish man on earth."

"Whatever it is, Gavin, just tell us." Trinity gently patted his arm.

"I don't want to win by default," Gavin said, wondering how his friends were going to take it. "I don't want Polly to turn to me just because she realizes she can't go with Travis. I don't want it to be like that. If she stays, if she chooses me in the end, I want it to be for me. I want it to be because she wants me as much as I want her. I don't want her to come to me heartbroken and looking for somebody to save her. I want her to come to that decision on her own and I know I will have to risk her walking off with Travis, but that is just the way it is."

"I don't understand," Dillon said, shaking his head vigorously from side to side.

"I think I do," Trinity said, and Dillon looked to her for an explanation. "You want her to love you for who you are, and not because you are a replacement, and that's it."

"Yes, that's it."

*a*s Polly made her way down towards the river, her steps got faster and faster. She knew she was cutting it fine and she had to get to Travis. If she wasn't careful, if she didn't hurry, she would arrive down at the river only to see his barge sailing away for the north and Portland.

She couldn't let him go, she knew it.

With everything that had rolled around in her mind day after day, finally everything had become clear. When Travis had told her that he was soon to go, everything suddenly slotted into place.

"I need your answer soon," Travis said the day before, just as he was taking his leave from the Whitaker farmhouse. "We're heading out tomorrow, and I won't be back."

"Is that really it? You really won't be coming back here?"

"I'll be getting my place in Portland and I won't be coming so far downriver on my new route."

"And you wouldn't visit?"

"What would be the point?" Travis looked downcast, his bright blue eyes seeming to cloud over with sadness. "You either want to marry me or you don't, Polly. You either want to start a life with me or you want to stay here with your folks, and that's it."

"It's just as simple as that, is it?" Polly said, and realized that it had been some days since she had spoken to him in angry tones.

"Of course, it is," he said, and stared into her eyes. He was so handsome. "Out there on the trail, you were ready to marry me at the side of the wagon train. You were ready to come with me into any kind of future. And I know now I should have married you there and then. I should never have risked losing you, and if I thought that our time apart would have changed your feelings so much, I would have taken you with me to California."

THE RIVERSIDE SEEMED to be a hive of activity. There were men darting to and fro, some carrying things, some shouting instructions to those already on the barge.

She already knew which barge Travis would be on, he'd walked her down to the river and shown it to her days before. It was enormous, so much so it almost took her breath away.

"Pardon me, Sir," she said, gently touching the arm of a man who had an authoritative look about him. "But I am looking for Mr. Travis Hurst."

"Are you now?" The man said with a broad grin, the sort of grin that left Polly wondering what it was he knew and she didn't. "Somebody give Travis a shout, would you?" He boomed at two of the men still standing on the barge.

Travis appeared in no time and, smiling happily, he climbed down off the barge and hastened towards her.

GAVIN DIDN'T CARE how suspicious he looked as he tried to keep himself out of Polly's sight down by the river. He knew that Travis's barge would be leaving that day and, if Polly was going to run off with her first love, Gavin had determined to silently see her off.

For some time, he'd hovered in the area and felt certain that Polly was nowhere to be seen. As time rolled on, Gavin began to nurse a hope that Polly had decided to stay right where she was, to stay there with him.

When he'd first seen her self-consciously making her way down towards the barge, her golden hair tied back in a ribbon and her pretty blue dress making her stand on the grain dust spoiled riverbank, he felt his heart sink. *So, she was going to leave with him after all*. Even though she had known all along what sort of man Travis was, still she was going to marry him.

For an awful moment, Gavin fought an almost overwhelming urge to go after her, to tell her every torrid detail he had discovered about the man she *loved*. He would, he knew, sacrifice anything, his own principles even, to keep her there.

But, in the end, he knew that Polly had to make up her own mind. And now that she had, Gavin would have to live with it.

"You're cutting it a bit fine," Travis said as he reached for her hand. "You sure do know how to give a man a scare. I've been peering out over the side of this barge for hour after hour, waiting for you to get here. I guess you're punishing me a little bit, huh?" Travis gave a mischievous chuckle, one which reminded her so much of times gone by, times out on the Oregon Trail when life was wonderful, for her at least.

"I didn't want to miss you," Polly said, and felt her stomach tighten into a great knot.

"I'm glad to hear it." Travis seemed truly happy.

As he stood there, his bright blonde hair at the top of a mighty frame, Polly knew that he was just about the most handsome man she'd set eyes on in all her life. She knew it out on the Oregon Trail, and she knew it now.

He was every bit as impressive at that moment as he had been on the day he had jumped down from his horse and lifted her up onto it so that she could take a little rest from walking beside the wagon train.

But that was it, and was all of it. That was as deep as her feelings for Travis went, and she finally realized that *that* was as deep as her feelings for Travis had *ever* been. They had been the almost childish feelings of first love, and they most certainly hadn't been the feelings of true love.

True love didn't care about a strong body, a handsome face, and blue eyes. It didn't care about fast-talking, winks, and mischievous grins.

No, true love cared about humor and caring. It cared about things in common and easy company. And it was true that she had all of these things in her life, she just didn't have them with Travis.

"Travis," she began, still nervous at the prospect of hurting him, despite the fact that she knew he had never given her a moment's worth of the same consideration.

"Come on then, let's roll," he said, laughing as if they were still on the Oregon Trail. "Otherwise, the barge will leave without the both of us."

"Travis, wait," she said, but he seemed determined to get on with it, to not listen to her at all.

"Hey, where are your things? Your bags, your clothes?" he asked, looking all around him for any sign of her possessions. "Did somebody already put them on the barge for you?"

"No, they haven't," Polly said, finally getting his attention. "And they're not going to. Travis, I'm not coming with you."

"What do you mean? What do you mean you're not coming with me?" His demeanor changed completely and she could see that he was shocked to the core.

Travis had assumed that he was still dealing with the girl who had begged him to take her with him that day at the Parting of the Ways. Despite his casual treatment of her, his lies about letters that were so obvious they were painful, *still*, he thought that she loved him so much she would put up with anything.

"Travis, I hope that one day you find a woman you can really love."

"But, I love…"

"No, you don't love me, Travis. You never did." She smiled at him, keen for them not to end on an acrimonious note. "But it was a lovely romance, really it was. I think we kept each other going out there on the Oregon Trail, didn't we?"

"It was more than that, Polly," Travis said a little darkly. He held her gaze as if trying to impress the veracity of his words.

"No, it wasn't." Polly took both of his hands in hers. "If it was, you would have written to me."

"But...." Travis trailed off, clearly realizing that she had never believed the lie.

"Take care of yourself, Travis, and have a wonderful life," Polly said with meaning before reaching up on tiptoe to kiss his cheek.


GAVIN COULD HARDLY BELIEVE what he'd seen. Had Polly kissed Travis's cheek and walked away from him? Was she just saying goodbye?

As Polly headed in his direction, Gavin stepped out from behind the pallet load of grain sacks he was sheltered by.

"Gavin?" she said, entirely shocked by his sudden appearance.

"Sorry, I didn't mean to startle you."

"What are you doing here?"

"I came to quietly say goodbye. I didn't want you to go without seeing you one last time."

"But I'm not going anywhere, Gavin." Polly smiled at him and reached out her hand.

"Why not?" Gavin had to know.

"I'm not going with Travis because I don't love him. I'm not sure that I ever really did now, maybe for some time." She shrugged. "But a lot can happen in ten months, I can hardly remember how it felt."

"I suppose things change over time, even feelings."

"Some do and some don't." She gave him a warm smile. "I don't think my feelings for you will ever change."

"I see," Gavin said glumly. "Well, I did tell you that I would be happy to be your friend forever, didn't I?"

"Oh, don't look so downcast!" Polly began to laugh. "What I'm trying to say is that it's *you* I love, and that won't change!"

"I see!" Gavin's heart lurched wonderfully. "I thought…"

"I know you did. And I guess I didn't give you cause to think otherwise. But I realized I could never leave you. I couldn't manage every day without your silly comments and your laughter. And it's real love this time, not love based on a handsome face."

"Wait a minute!" Gavin gave her his best mock-scandalized look. "Are you saying I'm not handsome, Miss Whitaker?"

"Well, I guess you're handsome to me." Polly was clearly enjoying herself. "Oh yes, and to Mrs. Taplow too. You are *devastatingly* handsome to Mrs. Taplow."

Gavin scooped her up without a moment's notice. Polly squealed with excitement as he spun her around and around.

"STOP IT, STOP IT, you crazy man!" she cried in excitement.

As he slowed to a staggered stance, the world seemed to carry on spinning around while they wobbled for a moment. "At least this close, you shouldn't be able to hit me too hard if I kiss you."

"Ha, you just try it…"

Before she could finish, Gavin had his lips pressed against hers, and the silence between them was just as it should be.

IN THE END, Gavin chose never to tell Polly all he'd found out from old drunken Jim in the saloon bar. She'd parted on good terms from Travis, and she had worked the man out for herself without moment's malice. That was good enough for Gavin, he didn't need to spoil things.

"I sure do love to put a meal together on a Sunday for everybody to come and enjoy," Polly said as she hastily chopped vegetables in preparation for when they returned from church.

"And you do very well, Mrs. Swain." Gavin stood behind his new wife as she continued to work and put his arms around her. "But tell me, do you think your mama is going to be bringing an apricot pie again?"

"I hope so," Polly said, without missing a beat.

"You really do hope so?" Gavin said, chuckling, and sounding surprised all at once.

"I sure do." Polly was also chuckling. "I just love to watch you trying to swallow down that dry pastry of my mama's, all the while trying to tell her just how much you're enjoying it. If I live to be a hundred-years-old, Gavin Swain, I'll never get tired of watching that little performance."

"Sounds to me like you don't have any regrets then?" Gavin kissed the back of her neck.

"Regrets that I didn't run off to Portland? No, not for a minute."

"Good," Gavin said with a grin. "And I don't think I have any regrets either."

"You don't *think?*" Polly wriggled in his arms and spun around to face him, her eyes wide and her mouth open.

"Of course, I don't have any regrets, Polly." Gavin laughed. "But if *I* live to be a hundred-years-old, I'll never get tired of teasing you."

"Believe it or not, I wouldn't have it any other way." Polly leaned forward and kissed him.

"I love you, Polly."

"And I *maybe* love you too, Gavin." She bit her bottom lip in mischievousness.

* * *

To FIND out when our next book is available join our exclusive newsletter and receive 2 FREE books http://amzn.to/2shQ9Ym

# PREVIEW OF CHARLOTTE'S STORY

This is the next book in the Pioneer Brides of the Oregon Trail Series. It is currently under final editing so please forgive me for any errors. I just wanted to share a brief excerpt with you as a thank you for reading this book.

"We are gathered here before God to witness the sacred union of Marlon Horton and Charlotte Clements." The Minister began.

Charlotte heard her name and almost panicked; she almost ran. If she went through with it all, she would be Charlotte Clements no longer. The last tie to her beloved Matthew would be severed forever.

Charlotte felt a tightness in her throat and knew she would have to put a stop to it. After all, Marlon would not be devastated; theirs was to be a marriage of convenience and nothing more. And that really would be it as far as Charlotte was concerned. Marlon meant nothing to her, she barely knew him.

He'd been kind and all, that was the truth, ever since her husband had died of Cholera just days before. But Charlotte couldn't think about anything at all, certainly not the man she was hastily marrying at the side of the great wagon train snaking its way to Oregon. And if she closed her eyes, she couldn't even begin to imagine what Marlon Horton looked like.

She'd seen him, of course, but she hadn't really studied him. She hadn't had enough room in her tortured heart to allow a single cell of the man to permeate, not even his appearance.

Charlotte closed her eyes up tight and tried to imagine him-- nothing came, just a vague impression of a man; an outline. Just a tall man with dark hair, no facial features or expression. No personality.

And then Matthew's face appeared so clearly in her mind that Charlotte almost cried out in pain. His handsome face was ashen pale and his soft brown hair hung limply plastered to the cold perspiration on his face.

When Carrie Easter, a lady whom some said was a doctor, had pronounced it to be cholera, Charlotte had known that the prospects for her husband's survival were slim to none. All she could do was tend to him as best she could, all the while trying to keep her little daughter safe and their wagon rolling.

There had been a number of illnesses and deaths along the way, and the wagon train could not stop for long. It just kept rolling ever forward and she knew there was nothing for it but to keep going, to keep trying.

All the while, as she tried to coax along oxen who were more used to her husband than her, Charlotte could do no more than think of the future they had planned for themselves out west and wish they had never attempted it.

They had sold up everything they owned back in Missouri so that they could start a new farm and a new life on the fertile soil of Oregon. That had been the promise. Nobody had told her that her beloved husband would not survive much past the River Platte and she would be forced to carry on into uncertainty.

"Do you have any family back east, Charlotte?" Marlon had asked her just that morning.

"No, nobody. And Matthew didn't have any folks left back home either. It was just the three of us." Charlotte spoke every word as if she was in a dream.

"I am a widower, Charlotte," Marlon spoke with purpose. "And I have been these last six months or so. It's what made me up and leave Missouri for Oregon."

"I'm so sorry," Charlotte spoke mechanically, her words having no real meaning in them.

All she knew of Marlon Horton was that he had been one of a number of people who had helped her over the immediate, difficult days since Matthew had died. Of them all, he had helped her the most, and helped her quietly.

Traveling with his twelve-year-old son, Marlon had gently urged her own oxen along in those moments when she had been unable to function any more, the moments when grief had her in its grip.

Charlotte had been well aware that Marlon's own wagon had been left in the care of his son while he helped her. With that in mind, Charlotte had been careful not to wallow in grief for too long. The truth was that she would have to put it to the back of her mind, become numb, until she arrived in Oregon.

"I was setting off for a new life in Oregon, I wanted to put some space between me and Missouri," Marlon had continued.

"I see." Charlotte wished that he would stop speaking.

"I realise it's not going to be easy to file a land claim and set up a house and farm on my own with my boy to look after."

"No." Charlotte's voice was barely audible as she thought of how she would manage exactly the same thing with a three-year-old daughter.

"And if it's not too much of an insult to you, I'd like to propose marriage. Not in the ordinary way, Charlotte, but in such a way that we can just help each other out."

"I see." Charlotte felt numb; she was still in shock and still married to Matthew in her heart.

"I know you're still in a bad way and I understand that same grieving and how rough it is, believe me. I'm not trying to take advantage, Charlotte, I'm trying to help us both." He paused for a moment. "I'm trying to do what's right by my own boy and I promise you I would help raise your daughter like she was my very own. These kids need two parents and a farm needs a partnership. It's not an easy thing to do alone, man or woman."

"That's true," Charlotte still spoke as if in a daze, never once really looking at Marlon.

Still, Marlon didn't seem put off by it and Charlotte was relieved; it took the pressure off her somehow. There was something in his whole demeanour which took the pressure off. There was no sense that he had any expectations of her, not even in matters of conversation and eye contact. No expectations at all. It was strangely soothing at a time when she hardly knew her left from her right.

And he was right; running a farm alone would be hard enough, but setting one up from scratch on virgin land would be near impossible. And that would be exactly what she would be doing.

None of it had seemed unachievable when she had Matthew at her side. As they had sat up night after night in their tent at the camp in Independence, Missouri, their excitement had squashed any doubts.

As they waited in the camp for the grass to begin to grow on the start of the Oregon Trail, the grass that would sustain the oxen for mile upon mile, nothing had seemed impossible.

They talked excitedly into the early hours of the land they would claim and the house they would build on it. They talked of living in their tent on their land until they had built their home and how they would set about plowing up their fields ready for sewing crops.

With Matthew by her side, Charlotte could have done anything. It was a new life, a hope for a more prosperous future for them and three-year-old, Katie.

"I don't think I can do it on my own," Charlotte said miserably as she finally turned her eyes upon Marlon Horton.

"I think we could both use a little help. I'm not offering to rescue you, Charlotte, and neither am I asking you to rescue me or to tend to my every need." Marlon had a very direct way of speaking. It was very open. "I'm suggesting a partnership if you like. We could marry and get one farm between us and share the work. We could raise the kids together and give them a chance of a family life again."

Charlotte thought of all she would have to do when she arrived in Oregon. There was no way she could build that house she and Matthew had talked about on her own, it just wasn't possible. She was no stranger to hard, manual work, but one person just couldn't build alone. And there was only enough money from the sale of all they'd owned back in Missouri to pay for the one-hundred-and-sixty-acre land claim and the materials for the house. Everything else they needed was due to come from the proceeds of their farm once it was up and running, that had always been the plan.

But how was she to do it all? When Matthew had died and been buried just days before, folk rallied around her, all keen to know if she was going to go forward or turn back.

Turning back just hadn't been an option; there was nothing to go back to in Missouri. No family, no home, no land. Everything she had was in that wagon, her livelihood included. Charlotte and Matthew had brought their best farming equipment with them and the wagon was fully laden. It had been a hard task to cross the River Platte, just as it had been for everyone. But she had done it with help. Matthew had been right there at her side.

While the going was flat as they crossed the immense plains, Charlotte knew that they still had the South Pass over the Rockies and the change in season to deal with as the terrain got harder again. How was she going to cope alone?

And when she arrived in Oregon, how would she build a house, start a farm, and look after a small child without any help? Charlotte felt so beaten; so dejected and utterly without hope.

She had never felt that way in her life. Charlotte had known hard times, that was for sure, but she'd never suffered so great and complete a loss as Matthew and didn't know how to keep putting one foot in front of the other.

She hadn't just lost her husband, she'd lost all their dreams and hopes for a happy, secure future. Everything had been buried in the ground at the side of the Oregon Trail with Matthew.

"Marlon, I accept your kind offer." Even as she had spoken the words, Charlotte felt sick.

Just days before she'd had a husband, and now she was due to have another one altogether. A stranger.

"I'll do right by you, I swear it," Marlon said and Charlotte could hear relief in his voice.

She believed him when he said that he was looking for a partnership, not a romance. He was still grieving himself, she could almost feel it. The relief, she felt sure, was the same as her own. It was the tiny spark of hope of not being entirely alone in the world. There was now another person in existence to turn to legitimately for help. Someone to lean on in both directions.

"I believe that, Marlon. And I will do right by you and your boy." Charlotte felt saved and doomed all at once.

"Then shall we make it official? I could run up along the wagon train a piece and look for the Minister? Or we can wait until the wagons are circled tonight and do it then?"

"The Minister might be busy when we stop for the day.

People always seem to need him when the day's walking is done," Charlotte said.

While this was true, she really thought they ought to get the Minister to perform the ceremony straight away before her heart had a chance to change her mind.

Charlotte didn't know if Marlon sensed it in her, but he set off immediately to hunt down the Minister, leaving a very sullen looking Clay Horton to keep the oxen moving. Charlotte knew the boy realized what was happening, unlike Katie who was sitting on the front of her own wagon smiling contentedly. She knew she ought to speak to Clay, to offer some sort of reassurance, but she couldn't; she didn't have it to give.

The brief ceremony seemed to have happened almost without her. Charlotte knew she had responded verbally wherever she was expected to, but she couldn't remember a thing about it.

"I now pronounce you husband and wife," the Minister said hurriedly, knowing the wagons would start rolling again any minute.

Marlon didn't kiss her and for that Charlotte was grateful. She stood unmoving, mourning the loss of her name; the name she had shared with Matthew for the last four years.

Just as she thought herself ready to cry, Charlotte felt a little hand in hers. She looked down to see Katie smiling up at her. Too young to be anything other than pleased and interested in the curious ceremony, Katie smiled up at her.

Of course, her last tie to Matthew was *not* severed. She had more of him than just his name and she would do forever. She had Katie, the most beautiful little girl in the world.

With a nod of thanks to the Minister and a smile to Marlon, Charlotte lifted Katie back up onto the wagon and made ready to set off again. She couldn't cry another tear, there just weren't any left.

To find out when Charlotte's Story is available join our exclusive newsletter and receive 2 FREE books http://amzn.to/2shQ9Ym

Nellie Clare was stirring the porridge, trying her hardest not to burn it, when her pa came into the kitchen. One look at him told Nellie that Leon Clare had already been out. His boots were covered in dust, and his hat was still on his head.

Nellie straightened up and flicked her long black ponytail back over her shoulders. Something was wrong. Normally Leon came downstairs after her, usually lured down by the smell of the food she cooked. He would eat his breakfast heartily before heading off to the mines where he was a foreman. Leon didn't like to roll out of bed until he knew breakfast was ready. Nellie knew this all too well and since her mother had died of pneumonia the winter before she had taken over the duties Ashleigh Clare had with regards to the house. This had included cooking a delicious breakfast to dangle the smell in front of Leon and keeping the house clean.

She didn't enjoy the cleaning, but she was a good cook. Leon was more than happy with food she offered, and so he let the cleaning issue slide. Nellie felt bad that she couldn't do it to the standards of her ma - her father was a very particular person when it came to the cleanliness of the house. So Nellie worked hard to keep things as best she could. As Leon was still distraught from losing his wife she wanted to make him happy.

Nellie made a cup of coffee and brought it over to Leon where he sat in his usual chair. She laid the steaming mug just out of reach as he had spread the newspaper he was studying out across the surface, almost covering half the table.

"Where did you go?" Nellie went back to the stove and checked on the porridge. It was bubbling nicely, so she took it off the heat and began to put it into two bowls. "You're not normally up this early. I didn't even hear you leave."

"Sorry, dear," Leon drawled, "I didn't know I had to ask permission."

Nellie stuck her tongue out at him. Leon laughed, his striking blue eyes so similar to her own, twinkled amongst the wrinkles of his face. He was actually looking a lot better than he had done in a long time.

"Actually, I went to get the paper." He patted the huge sheets. "They had just come in from the stagecoach."

"But you always get the paper." Nellie brought the bowls to the table, laying Leon's in front of him and setting a spoon beside it. "Why did you need to get it so early? There are always plenty left when you go after breakfast."

She sat to Leon's left and picked up the sugar bowl, spooning three large spoons onto the porridge before stirring it through. Leon frowned as she did this.

"I wish you'd stop using so much sugar. You're going to lose your teeth."

Nellie frowned. She knew Leon didn't like her sweet tooth. "You've never said anything about it before." She ate some porridge. "Anyway, it's my body. If I want parts to rot and fall off, that's my choice." She sweetened the words with a grin.

Food was a comfort to her. After all, there wasn't much for her in her hometown. At twenty-two, she didn't have any marriage prospects, and she didn't want any. The men in the mining town she had been born and grown up in were nice enough, but she couldn't see any of them as husband material. None of them saw her as wife material, either, so it didn't make her upset... she was happy to be as she was. Well, most of the time she was happy. Every now and then she would still have a childish dream of a handsome husband and children of her own. That was not to be, and she had to face life as it came.

Still, no one, not even her pa, told her what she could and couldn't put into her body.

Leon's frown deepened before it lessened and he looked down at the paper through squinted eyes, idly stirring his porridge.

"I went early because I wanted to make sure I got a paper." He ate slowly, his finger darting across the page. "Where is it? I saw you here earlier."

"Me... what... Pa?"

"Ah!" Leon tapped the page and looked up at Nellie triumphantly. "There it is."

Nellie leaned over and followed Leon's finger. She read the top of the section and her heart sank.

No. He wasn't. Was he?

"Matrimonial Pages - Mail Order Brides Wanted?" She stared at her pa with rising horror. "Pa, what are you doing buying a paper for this?"

Leon sighed. He rubbed at his eyes and pushed his porridge away.

"Look, honey, things are not brilliant in town right now. I want you to have a good life... and you're not going to get it here so..."

"You're marrying me off to a complete stranger?" Nellie's spoon dropped into her bowl. She stared at Leon, unable to believe what she was hearing. "Are you crazy? I told you that I was never going to do that. That's below me."

When she first saw a mail order bride advert she had been appalled. It was some frontier man in the Wild West looking for a woman in the east to marry and have a family with. Nellie had declared openly that she would never be one of those women. She didn't see it in a good light and Leon knew that. So to hear her father say he wanted her to go to the other side of the country to marry a man she didn't know... to leave him... it made Nellie feel sick.

"You say that but it works," Leon said earnestly. "Look at Prudence Langley. She's your age. She went out three years ago as a mail order bride, and she's been happily married ever since. Her mother says they've got one daughter and another child on the way."

"But she wanted to do that," Nellie protested. "I don't want to leave."

Looking genuinely upset, Leon reached over and took

Nellie's hand. Nellie pulled away. Leon's eyes narrowed, and his cheeks seemed to droop along with his shoulders.

"I'm sorry, Nellie. But we have to do something. You're twenty-two now, and none of the men around here have shown any interest in you."

"So what?" Nellie snapped back. "I thought you were going to leave me to my own devices with regards to that."

"I was." Leon paused. "Until I realized... when I saw those with grandchildren."

It clicked in Nellie's head. She stared at him.

"You want grandchildren? You've never said anything about it before." She harrumphed and slumped in her seat, her arms crossed over her chest. She knew she was acting like a child, but Nellie didn't care. She wasn't having it. "What about me, Pa? Don't I need to like the man I'm marrying? I could be marrying a madman, for all I know."

Leon snorted.

"Don't be ridiculous. Everyone's doing it. And they're not bad marriages." He leaned forward earnestly. "You can go elsewhere, have a family of your own, and not have me pulling you down."

Nellie didn't like it. In fact, she hated it. She didn't want to be put in this situation. The thought of leaving her father alone terrified her.

But she knew Leon Clare. Once he got his mind set on something, he wouldn't be dissuaded. This would be happening, whether she liked it or not.

\* \* \*

Sheriff James Taylor glanced at his new wife as he drove their cart up the hill to his home. She sat beside him, careful not to touch him, her head was down as she stared at her hands, which hadn't stopped fidgeting since he had helped her into the cart.

She didn't want to be here. Her body language made it clear. It looked like his marriage had started on shaky ground.

James couldn't understand why she had come if it was not what she wanted. When he had made the decision that it was time to settle down and start a family, James had been delighted that someone had actually written back to him. At thirty-three, he might have been considered a little too old for some people. The brides were usually eighteen, nineteen-years-old and would be nervous about having a much older husband. So when Nellie Clare had written back, saying she was twenty-two years old and she was interested in becoming his wife, James thought he had struck gold. It couldn't have got any better.

She wasn't bad to look at, either. If anything, she was very pretty. Long black hair she had tied in a chignon against the nape of her neck and startling blue eyes, as blue as the turquoise that was mined just outside Frye. She was slightly taller and slimmer in height and build than the average woman, but James preferred taller women. Petite women made him feel too big, even though he was barely six foot himself.

James had believed he had chosen well.

Yet there was something wrong. He could feel it. He had met her coming off the train, and they had gone straight to the chapel, just as they had discussed. There hadn't been much time to talk. James had just been eager to get married, then to take his new wife home and make sure nobody bothered them for a few days.

Now, going up to his home - their home - James could feel the tension. Things weren't adding up. There had been lots of enthusiasm in her telegrams and letters before they met and now there was virtually none. Nellie was quiet and barely spoke except to answer the priest when they made their vows. She didn't look at him, trying to look at anything and anyone else bar him. When his sister and a few close friends who had come to the sudden wedding as witnesses congratulated her, she was muted in her delight, but she conversed with them more than with him.

That hurt. James had expected a woman who wanted him. Now he was seeing a woman who looked to have been forced into this. She had turned her head away when it came time for the kissing of the bride, and James had had to settle for kissing her cheek.

James wasn't a forceful type of person, and he would never force this woman to be his wife if she didn't want it. Only now they were married and were stuck with it, come what may. James didn't believe in divorce, and he didn't have the heart to send her back to her home.

They were married, whether she liked it or not.

They reached James' house, he pulled the cart to a halt and jumped to the hard-dusty ground. A cloud rose around his feet and for a moment it filled him with gloom. He had been so excited about this day, and now he felt... betrayed. With a sigh he helped Nellie down, she pulled away from his hand as soon as her feet were on the ground. She waited on the porch while James put his faithful horse away, storing the cart beside the stall. He kept his distance, respectfully, when he returned, stepping around her to open the door before leading her inside.

"This is my place... our place." He stood near the door and allowed her to enter further into the lounge. "It's not much, but it is home."

It wasn't much, either. James had only purchased the house six months before. He had been living with his sister in their parents' house since they died but when Stephanie got married James didn't want to take up space they would need for a family. The furniture was simple, but it was sturdy. It wasn't very clean, but James didn't care; he was very rarely in with his job and only came back to sleep. Sometimes he didn't even sleep at home, he merely took a few hours at the sheriff's hut.

Now he wished he could have tidied up a little, so it didn't look so awful in Nellie's eyes. But he had been so eager to start a family and see his wife's belly swell with his child that he hadn't thought about the house.

Nellie let out a small snort as she looked around.

"It's a little untidy, isn't it?" Then she stiffened when she realized what she had just said. She turned to James, her hands going to her mouth. "Oh, I'm so sorry. That was..."

"A blatant observation." James chuckled. He shut the door and leaned against it with his thumbs hooked into the belt loops of his jeans. "I know it's not kept very well. I only moved in six months ago and with my work I haven't had time to set things straight."

"I take it being the sheriff is more than a full-time job."

"You could say that."

Frye wasn't bad, but there were a lot of people who liked their drink. Alcohol added to people usually meant fights. A lot of them. There weren't that many people here, either, so things got rather stretched when people got on top of one another.

James nodded around the lounge.

"Plus, with no housekeeper, it's just been collecting dust."

"I can tell." Nellie gave the room a rueful look around again. She grunted and turned back to him, her turquoise eyes clear but full of hurt. "I can see where this is going."

"How so?"

"You want me to clean for you. Do what I did back home."

Nellie's voice was tight as if she was trying to hold back her temper. James frowned.

"I'm not that experienced with wives but isn't that what they're supposed to do? Apart from the obvious?"

Nellie blushed. But she didn't look away.

"I looked after my father. I didn't say I was a housekeeper. And your ad read more like you were asking for a maid than a wife."

James arched an eyebrow. Was this what she had been expecting? He was confused.

"Then why did you say you would marry me?"

Nellie sighed.

"If you haven't noticed already, I can just about read, but I can barely write. My pa wrote to you, not me." She shook her head. "He said he wanted a better life and all but pushed the idea at me."

"And you want to make your pa happy."

That was all James needed. A father shoving his daughter into something she didn't want. He had thought he had found a good thing here... but all he had got was a nightmare.

Nellie closed her eyes for a moment. When she opened them, she looked like she had come to a resigned decision.

"The sooner I get this over with, the better." She bit her lip, but she didn't look away. "I'm sorry if that's not what you wanted to hear, but I don't want to stay quiet and build up resentment. You should hear it right at the start."

James was getting annoyed. While he appreciated you should have no lies in a marriage, he was frustrated that his ideas regarding his new wife had been dashed before they had even got to the wedding night. His wife wanted nothing to do with him and was only marrying him to please her father. That didn't sit well with James, that didn't sit well at all.

Between them, they had got him to marry her under false pretenses. James was mighty annoyed about that.

He nodded towards the stairs.

"Your trunk is in the master bedroom. Make yourself at home. I'll set my things up in the spare room."

"You're not sleeping in your room?" Nellie's voice sounded surprised. "With me?"

Was that some relief there? James gritted his teeth.

"I'm not a monster, Nellie. I'm not going to force myself on a woman." He turned away. "Get some sleep."

Then he opened the door and left, slamming the heavy wood so that it bounced in the frame behind him. What he wanted to do right now was get away and be alone. He didn't want to be anywhere near his new wife.

James set off across the dusty ground as the sun set before him. It could have been a romantic view to start their marriage properly... instead, what had he got? Some first day of married bliss this was turning out to be.

Find out how James and Nellie get on in this mega 36 book box set – 36 Cowboys and Brides FREE on Kindle Unlimited http://amzn.to/2wG5F7y

MORE BOOKS BY INDIANA WAKE

To receive two free Mail Order Bride Romance join Fair Havens Books exclusive newsletter. http://eepurl.com/bHou5D

**All Books are FREE on Kindle Unlimited**

**Newest Books**

**15 Brides of the Wild West – A Brides Cowboys and Babies Box Set**

**Trinity's Loss**

Carrie's Trust

Josie's Dream

**Hearts Head West**

No Going Back

A Baby to Heal his Heart

For the Love of the Baby

A Father's Blessing

A Surprise Proposal

**Mail Order Brides Out of Time**

Blackmailed by the Rancher

For Love or Duty

The Baby and the Beast.

Saving the Twins

A Dream Come True


**Box Sets**

**15 Brides of the Wild West – includes never before published book.**

**36 cowboys and Brides Mega Box Set with 5 never before published books.**

22 Book Mega Box Set – 22 Brides Ride West for Love

22 Book Mega Box Set – 22 Frontier Brides – Love & Hope Ride West http://amzn.to/1Xf8xNR

16 Book Boxed Set Love & Hearts http://bit.ly/1kXbkw4

10 Frontier Brides and Babies 10 Book Mega Box Set

10 Book Box Set 10 Healing Hearts

7 Brides for 7 lonely Cowboys box set http://amzn.to/1SXaQVG

An English Rose in Texas 5 Book Set 2 books never before published http://amzn.to/1Tl64iH

**The Mail Order Bride and the Marriage Agent Series:**

The Mail Order Bride and the Stolen Baby

Secret's Lies and a New Family

The Right Choice

The Mail Order Bride and the Hunted Man

His Golden Angel

Mistaken Trust

Love at Eighty Yards

The Narrow Escape

2 Book Set – A Celebration of life & No Sympathy

**Based on a True Story**

2 Book Special Into the Unknown& Call of the Hunter

**Novel Length books**

Christmas Hope & Redemption

Strength from Within – Anabella

The Wrong Proposal – Evelyn

A Leaf on the Breeze - Amelia

Nancy and Claudine Love Will Find You

# ABOUT THE AUTHOR

Indiana Wake was born in Denver Colorado where she learned to love the outdoors and horses. At the age of eleven, her parents moved to the United Kingdom to follow her father's career.

It was a strange and foreign new world and it took a while for her to settle down. Her mom raised horses and Indiana soon learned to ride. She would often escape on horseback imagining she was back in the Wild West. As well as horses, Indiana escaped into fiction and dreamed of all the friends she had left behind.

From an early age, she loved stories. They were always sweet and clean and more often than not, included horses, cowboys and most importantly of all a happy ever after. As she got older, she would often be found making up her own stories and would tell them to anyone who would listen.

As she grew up, she continued to write but marriage and a job stole some of her dreams. Then one day she was discussing with a friend at church, how hard it was to get sweet and clean fiction. Though very shy about her writing Indiana agreed to share one of her stories. That friend loved the story and suggested she publish it on kindle. Together they worked really hard and the rest, as they say, is history.

Indiana has had multiple number one bestsellers and now

makes her living from her writing. She believes she was truly blessed to be given this opportunity and thanks each and every one of her readers for making her dream come true.

Belle Fiffer is not your ordinary girl. She grew up in the west where she loved to ride horses and walk in the wilds. At fifteen, she moved to England when her father's job took him across the pond. Leaving behind all her friends she lost herself in books and if she is honest she fell in love with food. She is not ashamed of her curves and loves stories about good, honest men that love their women on the large side.

As a committed Christian, her books are clean, sweet and inspirational. Belle hopes you enjoy the books.

Made in United States
Troutdale, OR
06/11/2024

20475463R00072